A4

Singing on the *Titanic*

ILLINOIS SHORT FICTION

A list of books in the series appears at the end of this volume.

Perry Glasser

Singing on the *Titanic*

UNIVERSITY OF ILLINOIS PRESS

Urbana and Chicago

Publication of this work was supported in part
by grants from the Illinois Arts Council, a state agency,
and the National Endowment for the Arts.

This book is printed on acid-free paper.

"Away Out and Over," *Western Humanities Review,* Autumn 1978
"Easily and Well," *Colorado Woman Magazine,* January 1981
"The Last Game," *Ms.,* August 1984
"Marmosets," *Confrontation,* Spring/Summer 1986
"Singing on the *Titanic,*" *Woman's Day,* forthcoming
"Steering Clear," *North American Review,* forthcoming
"Visit," *Sucarnochee Review,* Spring 1985

Library of Congress Cataloging-in-Publication Data

Glasser, Perry.
    Singing on the *Titanic.*

    (Illinois short fiction)
    Contents: Mexico—Marmosets—Steering clear—
[etc.]
    I. Title.   II. Series.
PS3557.L348S5   1987   813'.54   87–1654
ISBN 0–252–01427–8   (alk. paper)

For Debi

Contents

Mexico

Here it was their second morning in Rocky Point, a town the Mexicans called Puerto Peñasco, and what Doralee Jackson wanted more than anything else in the whole world was a nice place with a real shower, something with hot water where she could shampoo the grit out of her hair and not feel like she'd been rolling in dust for three weeks, and what Kirk was doing at 7 A.M., the sun no higher than its own width out of the ocean, still reddish but turning yellow-white, was run into the water up to maybe his knees, then run out when a wave brushed by him, and then run in again.

Kirk wasn't even his real name. He'd told her his real name was Alexander Dugan when they were someplace in Oklahoma or maybe it was Texas, and he told that to her like he was letting her in on some great secret and she should feel grateful. All she could think was to ask herself what was she doing there in the front seat of a blue '78 Nova with the cattle stink blowing in the car window with a guy whose name was one thing but who wanted to be called another. "But you keep calling me Kirk," he'd said, " 'cause I'm a Kirk. No woosy Alex." And he reached under the seat to pop another can of Lone Star and then he'd squeezed her knee.

Kirk wore just his Levi's—no socks, shoes, shirt, or underwear, she knew—and each time he ran into the water he went a little farther before he ran out, like a kid working up his courage for the plunge. With a warm can of Carta Blanca in her hands, Doralee sat on the Chevy's hood, her bare feet flat on the metal getting hot from the sun, and she looked at her own knobby toes, or watched the waves roll in

and smooth over Kirk's footprints on the dark wet sand. Carta Blanca
for breakfast was bad enough, but warm it tasted like piss. They hadn't
eaten since lunch yesterday and the beer was making her fuzzy. She'd
have taken a box of good American corn flakes, even. She'd eat them
dry.

She liked the Mexican beach. It was a big dirty yellow crescent of a
beach and they were right in the middle. When she looked to the left or
right she had to squint, and way out at the ends of the crescent, haze
from the ocean made it hard to see clear, but she knew there was more
beach and little patches of grass and weeds. Hardly any people at all
except for some Mexican kids that were poking around in the sand off
by a beat-up white house, looking for something they could steal, she
bet. The salty wind that blustered and snatched at her hair carried their
voices, the sound not much different from the birds she thought were
pigeons until Kirk told her they were pelicans, stupid. Well, how could
she know? It was the first time she'd seen the sea, just a big lake where
you couldn't see the other shore.

In Mexico not two days and she already knew that Mexico was
dumb-ass as a place could be. It was crazy weird how they let you drive
right up on the sand. Nice, but all the cars and vans and campers
leaked oil and in the sun that crap turned into tar, so when a body
walked barefoot the gunk got all sticky on the soles of her feet. Yesterday, Kirk soaked a rag with gasoline and wiped her feet clean. She was
amazed how easy it was. Kirk knew stuff like that.

"Are you going in the water or not?"

He didn't answer, but took another run, the water splashing up
around him, his jeans dark where they were wet but light blue above
the knees, and this time when he got in as high as his waist he lunged
head first forward in a kind of half-assed dive and broke a wave. For a
second he was invisible under green water and then he shot up, waving
his skinny arms in the air, shaking his head so his long hair swirled wet
slapping around his face. A wave followed him in and his footprints
were washed flat. Water streamed off him. His feet were caked with the
whiter dry sand of the beach. He wiped his face with his palm.

"I could do with some food. I'm hungry, Kirk."

"We'll eat. I told you, we'll eat. Let me dry off, then we'll walk
through town and see what we can find. We out of cupcakes?"

"Ate the last ones yesterday lunch."

"Shit."

He took his black T-shirt from the car's front seat and wiped his chest, then his arms, rubbing carefully at the spot where the faded tattoo of the Zig-Zag man was. His black hair was all matted, and when he rubbed his head with his T-shirt his hair didn't look any drier, but was strung out in thick, knotted strands, like the hair on a nigger in some Jamaican reggae band. He smoothed it back with his hands, two, three times, and then snapped it into a ponytail with a red rubber band.

"Gimme some of that." He took the beer from her, filled his mouth by leaning his head way back, then gargled and spit. "I figure two, three days, Dora. Two, three days, and someone around here will notice us, and we score some dope. Run it back across the border. Los Angeles, Las Vegas, maybe. We sell it, and we're all right. Do whatever we want, then."

"I don't know, Kirk. This place doesn't look right."

"I been wrong so far?"

"No." She had to admit it.

"I'm telling you, there's dope all over Mexico. That's all these greasers do. Brown heroin. Grass. Hell, we get lucky, someone will offer us coke. All we got to do is hang around until someone picks up on us and tries to sell us a couple of joints. We tell him we're in the market for a couple of kilos. Next day, we're out of this pisshole."

Rocky Point was a fishing village. When they'd first driven through the town Doralee was amazed by the posters on the corrugated metal sides of some of the buildings. Neither of them read Spanish, but the posters showed a big face above a red hammer and sickle. Wasn't communism illegal or something?

Kirk had picked the town because he wanted to swim in the ocean, and Rocky Point was close to the border, was on the Gulf of California, and on the map looked like an itty-bitty drive south from Arizona that had turned into hours and hours over the goddamndest emptiest desert in all of Creation, just sky and land, big brown hump-backed hills with nothing on them but lizards and sick little bushes, the car like an oven even at seventy miles an hour with the windows open. They had been in Tucumcari, New Mexico, the night he picked the town right off a map. He could have thrown a dart.

Doralee kept her doubts to herself. Maybe he hadn't been wrong yet, but she wasn't convinced he was absolutely on the money much, neither.

And she wanted him to be right. This was a shot, and she wasn't ready yet to give up on Kirk Dugan even if his real name *was* woosy Alex.

In New Mexico, Kirk had had three hundred-dollar bills folded small, and he'd pried the heel off his left boot, put away the bills, and with the butt end of the Browning automatic tapped the heel back into place. Then they'd driven way the hell south and way the hell west, charging gas and whatever they could buy to eat in truck stops or gas stations on the MasterCard Kirk took off a guy in Oklahoma named William Krantz, driving day and night until they were in something called the Organ Pipe Monument in Arizona, and a few miles from the border he stopped the car, got out to take a whizz, and walked with her a dozen or so yards from the road. They were at the 3 mile marker on the west side of the road. She'd never seen so many cactuses, big things with arms just like in a picture book. And it was quiet, no sound of any kind, and she thought that was spooky for a place called Organ Pipe. Kirk told her to look around, remember what the spot looked like, and then he scratched an X on a big white rock. He lifted the rock. Two scorpions, little orange things with tails curled in the air, scuttled out.

"Jesus fucking Christ!" Kirk yelled and dropped the rock. He stamped the scorpions. Lifted his foot and brought his boot down hard, again and again, till they were so flat they were nothing but dust, and then he lifted the rock again, scraped a little depression in the spot under the rock, put the gun in the plastic wrap from a loaf of white bread, and left the gun under the rock. You don't want to go over the border with a gun, he explained, but whether that would matter if they were caught with a car full of marijuana was something she didn't ask him.

So here she was, her second day in Mexico. Kirk pulled his black boots on over his socks and then pushed his head into his shirt. He touched his jaw, made the kind of face that showed he knew he needed a shave, something he did every three days or so if they could find hot water and a bar of soap.

"The shirt'll dry on my back," he said. "What do you say? Let's look around. I'm starving."

Doralee smiled. He was the goddamndest thing to make her smile, except the times he scared her to death.

They locked the car and walked up the hill into the town, which wasn't all that big. There was one straight street that ran along the cement docks from where fishing boats had already gone out, and the street stank like hell from the offal right there on the ground, the flies buzzing so loud you could hear the noise a hundred yards away. And behind that street were a bunch of little narrow streets that climbed the face of what could be a big hill or a small mountain—she didn't know what to call it, there was nothing like it back in Iowa—and those streets twisted and turned on each other so quick a body got lost faster than a rat in one of those mazes. They went up the hill, Kirk smoking and getting winded but trying not let Doralee see that, but she could hear him wheeze and when he stopped two times to look in a store window she knew he was just catching his breath.

He smoked Marlboros, the red pack tucked into the waist of his jeans. He smoked all the time. She'd never known a man to smoke as much as Kirk, sometimes up in the middle of the night to smoke a cigarette and then right back to sleep. She'd wake from the stink or his movement, and she'd see the orange glow of the tip in the darkness and she'd watch that, just that, and never let on that she was awake. And then Kirk would fall back and go to sleep again and she had to lie in the darkness with the burning stale smell settling into her hair and lingering in her nose and it would take a long time before she could sleep again.

They climbed the hill, but then the street turned and they couldn't go up the hill anymore, and the street took them back to the Coca-Cola sign. The third time that happened, Kirk picked a street that didn't go up but seemed to run parallel to the shoreline and the docks down below, and they passed a few closed restaurants that through the dark glass looked like luncheonettes, and then they got lucky, they could smell it before they saw it, they found a bakery. There were sleigh bells on the door.

The woman who came out of the back and stood behind the glass counter was as wide as she was tall, and she spoke no English but smiled a lot. She put one of each thing they pointed at on the counter-top. There was no beer, so Kirk took a carton of milk and placed it with the rest of the food.

"How much?" Kirk said and waved his hand over the three loaves and the milk that were on top of the counter.

The woman smiled.

"Dumb shit," Kirk said. "How much?" He raised his voice. "Pesos?"

"*Si, si.*"

"Just give her some money. Lord, doesn't it smell great?" It did. The thick aroma made Doralee feel warm and good, and for the first time in two days she thought maybe things had a chance to work out.

"I don't want to get cheated."

"She's not going to cheat you."

"They all cheat you down here."

The woman was nodding her head, smiling. Doralee'd bet she thought they were married or something, honeymooning. She smiled back at the dark, fat woman.

"Damn," Kirk said, and he pulled a wrinkled dollar bill, still wet, from his pocket and passed it over the counter. The fan in the corner whirred. They waited while the woman went to the back, heard her talking to someone, and then came back with a bunch of bills in her hand and a few coins. She put the bread in a sack. Kirk took the money and waited for Doralee to grab the bag and the milk, and they left the place, the little bells ringing when they went out the door. They walked maybe a half block, then sat on the curbstone, the bag between them.

The bread was heavy, the crust hard, and when Doralee broke one, the very white inside steamed. It was delicious, and the milk was creamier than any kind she'd ever had from a carton back in Iowa. "This is great," she said. Her teeth savagely ripped into the bread.

"Look at this," Kirk said. He held the money out to her.

"What about it?"

"Fucking Monopoly money." He counted it. "We've got thirty pesos and some centavos. Red bills and blue bills and I don't know shit about these coins. Feel 'em. They feel like tin."

"Isn't this bread outrageous?"

"What in fuck am I going to do with a pile of play money?"

From across the street, two skinny boys watched them eat. They were maybe ten, Doralee thought. Shouldn't they be in school? They had jet black hair and jet black eyes, and their eyes were enormous.

"Look at those kids," she said and swallowed a soft lump of the doughy bread. "They're cute."

Kirk flipped one of the coins. It hit the cobblestone street, making a thin sound. He picked up the coin. "It's about the size of a quarter," he said, "but it doesn't weigh as much. You think I could use it in a machine back home? You know, get a game of Donkey Kong with it or something? Cigarettes? Or you think the weight won't let it work?"

The two boys continued observing them. They weren't so cute, she decided. They were spooky. They didn't blink. Hardly moved. They ought to be in school. Learn something and clean up this shitty little town when they got older. She never saw a place so filthy. She shifted her weight. When one of the little boys tapped his friend's shoulder and they ran off down the street, she was glad, but then she got depressed. The feeling she'd had in the bakery was gone. This would never work out. A full belly helped, but this time Kirk was out of it. No town with kids running around on the street staring at them because they had food and money was going to cough up a dope dealer that would sell them anything worth anything. There was nothing in this town you could buy, much less sell.

"You listening to me?"

"I heard you."

"Well, what do you think?"

"I don't know. I guess you'd have to try it."

He snorted. "That's you all the time."

"What?"

"Never mind."

"What's that supposed to mean?"

"Drink your fucking milk."

The sun was higher and it was getting hot. Sweat trickled from under her arms and down her ribs. They finished their breakfast. She had to wait while Kirk smoked another cigarette. Some mornings when they'd been on the road she'd wake up to hear him coughing in the bathroom of the motel room—the room compliments of Mr. William Krantz—and she thought Kirk was like to die. He'd spit into the toilet and then he'd piss, the door of the bathroom open, sounding like a horse passing water.

They walked down to the dock where some of the boats were already in. Kirk said these guys had it easy, a job done for the day so early in the morning. She saw it wasn't fish but shrimp they caught. "Dollars," the fishermen said. "Five dollars, eight pounds," and they smiled their greasy smiles. When Doralee and Kirk walked away, they sometimes ran after them, and one guy yelling "Ice! Ice!" put his hand on Kirk's shoulder, but Kirk spun around so fast the man got scared and went right back to the counter where with little curled knives they cut the shrimp apart, scraping stuff right off the wood into the street, and there must have been a million gulls flocking in, picking at the stuff with their beaks, pulling, and shredding the leavings. The smell was getting to her, but it was not so bad now that with a full belly the fuzziness from the beer was gone.

Back toward the car on the beach, they passed a street they had not noticed before, one that ran along the beach in the other direction, what seemed away from the cluster of buildings on the hillside, and Doralee said, "Let's explore," and Kirk at first said no, and then seemed to think about it a minute and then shrugged his shoulders and said, "Why not? Maybe this is where the dealers hang out."

The long straight street was wider than the others, and it was paved with blacktop, not cobblestone. Kirk played with the Mexican coins still in his fist, jingling them, the sound funny to their ears, not like real money. Trees were on the street, tall scraggly things that were not growing well, but still were honest-to-God trees, and then the street turned one way and then another, and they were practically walking on top of a seawall, the waves crashing into the abutment, covering huge black rocks slimy with algae at the wall's base and sending up a spray of sea water. And at the end of the street through an open black iron gate were four buildings set in a square around what must have once been a fountain, though now it was dry and covered with the same brown dust that covered everything else in Rocky Point.

Kirk started to walk away, like they'd come to the end of the road. Looking out over the seawall they could see across the water over to the curve of the beach where the Chevy reflected the bright sun from its windshield. He was like that, she'd learned, wanting to keep near things he knew, so Doralee had had to grab him by the hand and they walked all the way up to the place. Above the iron gate, in letters that once had been bright blue paint but were now so faded they were almost invisible on the pale brown wall, were the words "La Hacienda." And as they got close enough to read those letters, Doralee saw that in the courtyard parked in the shade beneath the second-storey walkway were several dust-covered cars with American license plates, mostly California, but one or two from Arizona.

"It's a motel," she said, sounding to herself a little like she'd just discovered a lost gold mine or something.

"Good guess," Kirk said. "Let's go back to the car."

"I want to stay here. We can get a room."

"We can't take a fucking room here. We're here to score dope. You want to spend that money on a fucking room?"

But she pulled him further into the courtyard past the gate, and pasted on a glass door to what had to be an office that could not have been seen from the street was the MasterCard symbol.

"I want to stay here, Kirk. You can be William Krantz."

"I told you, that card's getting too hot. Every day we hold it, it gets hotter."

"Then what good is it?"

"Maybe we can find some asshole give us a hundred dollars for it. It's near ten days, now. The number is out."

"Even in Mexico?"

He looked at the building, the stark shadows falling black over the courtyard. A housemaid pushed a cart loaded with clean linen along the second-storey walkway. "Maybe not. I guess they get the word slower down here."

"Well, then, why not?"

"We aren't going to meet any Mexicans here. Just grampas from California. It doesn't make sense."

"You think we'll meet a dealer on the beach?" She grabbed his arm and put her face up close. This was no time to be chicken. "I want a shower. I need a shower."

"Listen, two, three days, I swear it, we'll be going to Las Vegas. You ever been in Las Vegas? We'll have the stuff and we'll unload it in Las Vegas. Just hang on."

"Kirk, this is a fucking fishing village, not goddam Acapulco. Which one of them fishermen you figure is the cocaine dealer in disguise? There were any dope dealers in this fucking town, one or two of these places might have had a paint job once or twice the past twenty years. I want a goddam shower. Is that asking too much?"

"You're losing faith, babe. I'm telling you, everybody in Mexico deals dope."

"How do you know that? Just how do you know that?"

"This guy said."

"What guy? What guy? I've heard about this guy a lot now. Who was he?"

"Lower your voice. You want the whole world should hear you?"

"What guy?"

"Just a guy I knew."

"When? Where?"

"He was a guy."

She watched him chew his lip, then tap his teeth with his fingernail. She had to say it. He scared the shit out of her, but not that much. "There was no guy, was there?"

"Sure there was."

"What was his name?"

"I forget. Just a guy."

He couldn't bullshit worth a damn. He wasn't going to say it, but she was sure, now. There had never been a guy. It was a dream. Talk about your Mexico, your dope, your dealers, your smuggling, or your selling, and Kirk knew bubblefuck.

"All right. There was a guy. That's terrific. But I tell you, Kirk, I am not doing my business squatting over the fucking sand. You don't want to stay here, fine. You take me somewhere else. Anywhere you like. But I'm not spending another night in that car on the back seat, you hear?"

"You're changing," he said. His eyes were darker. "You weren't like this back in Iowa."

"Fuck you."

She'd always been like this; he just didn't know it. The first and only time in her life she'd relaxed and allowed a man to take charge, she was begging for a toilet.

He was smiling now. "You're changing, all right."

"Are we going to stay here or not? 'Cause if you say not, I'm leaving."

"Just where you going to go? Tell me that."

Damn. "I'll hitch."

"You'll hitch. In Mexico. Through that fucking desert."

"I swear, I'll do it."

"You'll be raped and dead in twenty-four hours."

"I'll take my chances."

He paused. "I believe you would, babe. I believe you would." He lighted a cigarette with the silver-turquoise butane lighter he'd shoplifted in a truck stop outside Amarillo, inhaled deeply, and closed his eyes. "Well, I guess Mr. William Krantz can spring for one or two more nights. He hasn't complained yet."

She started to hug him, then thought she'd better not. It would tell him something she didn't think was true anymore, something she was learning more and more, something she did not want him to know.

She'd taken her chance and here she was, and nothing was the way it was supposed to be because Kirk Dugan was a lot more asshole than she had guessed, and the truer that got then the closer to the notion that she had not been too bright herself to hook up with him had to be reckoned with. She'd never thought Doralee Jackson the smartest girl in Des Moines, but she sure as shit was not the dumbest, though it was starting to look that way. If she kept her eyes sharp, she'd see the way out. Keep her fingers crossed, mouth shut, and spread her legs only enough to keep him happy, because if he wasn't happy he'd as soon leave her as take her, so where she had set out for a good time and a nice ride, now she would have to concentrate on getting out with her skin.

Things could get real basic on you. Bread, milk, the ocean, the wind, and survival. Basic. Hell and damn, she used to be smarter than this.

She was awful glad that gun was under a rock in Arizona.

When Doralee Jackson was nine years old her Momma one night gathered her and her two younger brothers up in her arms, ran them out of the house to a taxicab, and took them to the shelter where they lived for two whole months before Momma was sure enough the injunction she got from the judge would really and truly keep Poppa away. Doralee didn't miss Poppa one little bit, and she never told Momma or anybody else about the two times he'd come to her in the night when she was eight and explained exactly what good girls did and kept their mouths shut afterward. Momma didn't miss Poppa much, neither. The swelling on her face went down and she turned into a downright pretty woman once she learned how to take care of her hair, got some clothes, and quit the beer.

The people from the shelter got them an apartment on the southeast side of Des Moines, what was called the Bottoms, and they must have given Momma some training because Momma got a job first as a wait-ress and then as a cashier at the Denny's out near the interstate. Dora-lee didn't remember much about those times right after the shelter, just especially how she would be alone and had to take care of her brothers Jimmy and Daniel, making peanut butter sandwiches and when she got to be a little older defrosting fried chicken TV dinners night after night. It wasn't so much taking care of the boys she remembered, but the being alone in the darkness waiting for Momma, the boys asleep, watching the black-and-white television that stood on the kitchen table, expecting anytime that Poppa would show up at the front door and take them away. But he never did, and Doralee never learned just where he'd gone to, and that was just fine with her.

Momma slimmed down, and by the time Doralee was thirteen she understood why there were nights Momma didn't come home at all, or if she did come home made it in at three or four o'clock in the morn-ing. She was having her time, and she was entitled to it, didn't Doralee think? Momma would ask her when they both had a cup of morning coffee in the half-hour before Jimmy and Daniel got out of bed, Mom-ma's lipstick leaving rings on the rim of the cup that later Doralee would have to scrub to get rid of. Momma told her about the truckers that came into the restaurant and how nice some of them were, the Southerners the most gentlemenlike, fellas who'd been to faraway places with names that sounded to Momma (and to Doralee) like places from a storybook. Iron City was Pittsburgh, Bean Town was Boston, and the Music City was Nashville, of course. And there were places that didn't have nicknames, like Des Moines, but sounded nice when you said or heard them (not like Des Moines which didn't sound to Doralee or Momma like nothing at all). Joplin, Missouri. Wichita, Kansas. Bakersfield, California. And the cabs of some of the trucks in the little space behind the driver's seat were fixed up like little apartments, with stereos, a place to sleep, pictures on the wall, even. It was a wonder how those truckers got so much into so tiny a space.

A body might expect all of this to have gotten in the way of Doralee's schooling, but the fact of the matter was that it didn't make much difference at all. Doralee and schooling never had all that much to say to each other. She could read good enough, and she could do her arithmetic, but beyond that school somehow seemed not to be the main thing. They called her "Dumb Dora," of course, but she took that in stride because it came from the kids who didn't know much about real life, like how to cook what you bought at the 7-Eleven, what to do when your little brother burned his hand on the radiator, or how to give your Momma just enough brandy when she had the cramps. *That* stuff never showed up on those tests where you had to fill in the itty-bitty circles with your pencil. She knew what she knew, and she suspected that if the tests had questions about things that mattered, she'd do just fine.

The day she turned seventeen she went to the counselor at school and said she was ready to quit, and the counselor sort of shrugged his shoulders like that might not be such a bad idea. Momma thought it was all right, too.

She went on mornings at the supermarket and looked for an afternoon job, and quick enough got one at the Burger King right near the South Ridge Mall. She hated the stupid polyester uniform, and she had to cut her hair because she wouldn't wear a net on her head, but it was another twenty hours a week. She brought home french fries to reheat for Jimmy and Daniel—they were growing up pretty good and she didn't worry about them anymore, Jimmy good enough at varsity football there was a chance he might go to college the coach said if he didn't hurt himself, and Daniel getting along in junior high. Momma seemed to be slowing down, a steady fellow that had lasted more than a year, now, though Doralee had a hunch he was married someplace or

other because Momma clammed up about him whenever Doralee
hinted around that. She waited six months and then announced to
Momma that she was moving into her own place.

"I'm nearly eighteen," she said.

"You're a baby."

"I ain't never been a baby, ever."

That remark made Momma cry, something she did more and more
lately. Doralee was sorry for that, but she couldn't help any, now could
she?

But she hadn't been asking permission or for approval, and so soon
enough she found an apartment on the third floor of a five-storey walk-
up. Two rooms that weren't much, but they were furnished, they
wanted only a half-month's rent security which would leave her some
left over to get linens and plates and whatever, and the place was real
close to the bus lines she needed to get to her two jobs.

There had been boys, but they had not been important, what with her
not having a lot of time on her hands to go riding in some redneck's
pickup and park by Gray's Lake or the Saylorville dam. She knew she
didn't look like any damned Hawkeye cheerleader whose shit smelled
like ice cream, but she was far from ugly. Her figure was all right, her
belly flat, and it seemed to stay that way no matter what she ate. She
might have asked for a little more on top, but she did all right with
what she had.

Ricky Laughton took her out now and then, a boy she knew from
when she was in high school who one day when she still lived with
Momma had walked through her checkout aisle and recognized her. He
came back a day later to buy just a loaf of bread, and she knew right
away he was sweet on her because he could have gone through the
speed aisle but instead waited on line with just the one loaf of bread
under his arm. He'd take her bowling, they'd have some beers, and
once he took her roller-skating, but after a little time they would run
out of things to say, and she could predict that soon as the conversation
dried up he'd take her home and park a half-block from the building
where Momma lived, and then he'd try to kiss her. She'd let him, now
and then, but she didn't get any feeling from it, and he never tried to do
much else, which was fine with her.

Art Phillips tried to do more. He worked with her at the supermarket, and the very first time he was with her got himself so worked up she almost laughed. He was so serious, smelling of Aqua Velva and hair tonic but still smelling green and wet as the lettuce and cukes he worked with all day long in produce, and he spent the whole Clint Eastwood movie fiddling with the buttons of her blouse, trying to jack-knife his hand under her bra, and her all the time keeping her eyes straight ahead on the movie, making like she didn't even know his arm was wrapped like a snake around her neck. When he took her home she practically jumped out of the car before he could turn off the engine, ran into the building where she lived, and leaned against the door while she laughed. He asked her out again, and the second time she played hard-to-get, not so much because she wasn't sure if she liked Arthur well enough, but because she had spent a week trying to figure out if she were a virgin or not. Did what her father had done count? So the third time Arthur took her out—another movie, it was the only thing he could think of—after the movie he bought a six-pack and she let him take her north of the city, halfway to Fort Dodge. It was May, and it was warm. There was moonlight of sorts. They drank the beer, and she let him do it to her in the back seat of the car so she wouldn't have to wonder about it anymore. She liked it all right, and she did it with Arthur one more time to be sure, and while he was going at it she was thinking about the green-checked café curtains she had seen at Montgomery Ward that might go nice over the little window she had in her bathroom.

Two years passed. There were a few other boys, even one or two she could properly call a man, and while she gave herself away now and then, she kept a rein on it, too. She hoped for a man who offered a little excitement. Some part of Doralee still heard the music in those names of places that were far off, those places that Momma's truckers had talked of. Tulsa. Yuba. Chino. Denver. Houston. Corpus Christi. Albuquerque. Doralee Jackson was mired in Des Moines, Iowa, the heart of the toolies, which wasn't the end of the earth, but if you had a mind you could throw a rock off the edge.

The jamokes she came across chewed tobacco and wore adjustable hats that said John Deere on the crown, and it seemed if she let them

into her pants they all either disappeared or started right away talking
about children and putting in one hundred fifty acres of soybeans and
did she want to settle down? Which she most certainly did not. She was
not one of these fluff-brained beauties that thought of a man as something that would take care of her forever and ever. No, thank you very
much, Doralee Jackson would damn well take care of herself. She
wasn't good at much, but she was damned good at that.

She was nineteen when Kirk Dugan came into the Burger King and
she was working the second register on the right. He ordered the
chicken sandwich, a Dr. Pepper, and the large fries, and she hardly
looked up, would not have noticed him at all, except that when she gave
him change for a five he said,

"I gave you a ten."

She checked the register—she was careful with money—and there
was no way he had given her a ten-dollar bill. If he thought so, he was
wrong. But she checked, then did a check of the register tape against
the cash drawer, running totals, and told him he had given her a five.

He raised his voice the slightest bit, said he would call the manager,
what did she think she was doing to him?

"Listen," she said and noticed his black hair, stubble of beard, and
blue eyes, so when she started out stern despite herself her voice got
soft, "I'll get you the manager if you want. His name is Duncan, but
he's going to do what I just did which is to check the receipts against
the drawer, and I'm telling you, you gave me a five. Why don't you just
sit down and enjoy your sandwich? There're other people waiting."

And that was when he smiled and muttered, "Shit, can't blame a
man for trying," and she'd had to laugh when he walked away, looking
more sorrowful than a dog in a drought.

She forgot about him, but two hours later when her shift was up and
she was ready to leave, she stepped out in front and there he was, still
sitting at a table, still sucking on the straw in the same Dr. Pepper.

"You need a ride home?"

"The buses run."

"You don't have to be like that."

"I sure do," she said and went to the bus.

While she walked to the bus stop he drove a white Ford flatbed real
slow right next to her, the window rolled down so he could talk, him

leaning all the way across the seat not watching at all where he was going, the other cars coming around the truck honking their horns, but he didn't seem to mind. She noticed the truck had Illinois plates.

"You're not from around here," she said.

"How'd you know that?"

"I could tell."

At the bus stop he parked and she stood, waiting. She thought he was cute in a rough way. She wasn't at all scared.

"I'm just passing through town for a day or two. Made a delivery. My name's Kirk. Kirk Dugan. You're Doralee."

There was no sign of the bus. It was due in a minute. "You read my name tag."

"That's right. What's your last name?" The flatbed's bad idle made it rattle and cough. Kirk bent toward her and the door swung open. "I could take you home, Doralee."

The bus rumbled up to the stop, and the driver gave Kirk a blast of his horn. Doralee got on the bus, and the whole ride home kept herself from looking out the bus windows to see if the flatbed was following the bus, and when she got off she expected to see it, but it was not there. Walking up the three flights of steps to her place, she didn't know if she was relieved or disappointed.

A month or so later, about fifteen minutes before quitting time at the Burger King, Kirk Dugan showed up again, waiting on line at her register even though the one next to hers was open and twice the girl said, "Can I help someone?" He ordered just a Dr. Pepper, smiled at her, and gave her the exact change. Never said a word except to order. At quitting time she walked into the parking lot, her uniform stinking of the smell of cooked beef, and she looked for the flatbed, but it wasn't there, so she started out for the bus stop and that was when she heard her name called. She hadn't seen him because he was in a blue Chevy Nova, slouched way down low in the seat. The Chevy had Iowa license plates. She went to the car.

"You remember me?" he asked.

"Fella from Illinois. Kirk Dugan," she said, and the minute she said his name realized it was a mistake to do so, because then he knew she'd thought about him. He smiled broadly, knowingly. There wasn't any point, then, to stalling, so she went right around the car and got in. The front seat was covered all over by cigarette ashes and crumpled pieces of cellophane. He started the car, making the tires squeal just like she knew he would, and she directed him to her place.

They parked right in front of the walk-up where she lived and he asked if he could see her the next day, now that he knew her address.

"You just passing through?"

"Noper. I'll be here a bit, this time. Got a job. Knew a fellow who knew a fellow, so here I am."

"Doing what?"

"Pump gas. A little mechanical work. Been in town couple of days, got this car, and the guy lets me bunk in this trailer they got out back, until I find a place, he says. How about it? You want to go for a ride with me tomorrow?"

"Ride where?" Doralee knew she was going to say yes, but not quite yet. She saw no harm in it, and the car did have Iowa plates.

"Well, I don't know. I don't know. I was hoping you'd have some ideas about that. I don't know my way around here at all."

He looked so damned confident she wanted to scream, but he was acting like a gentleman, so she said it would be all right if he called for her at 7:30, and he did, the next night. That first time together she let him put his hand in her pants after they kissed some, and in a week he was coming by for her at work every day at the end of her shift, and pretty soon she believed she was in love with him, not for anything he said or did, but just because he had a way about him that made her feel easy with him. He told her about his times in Illinois, how he had been in what he called a boys' school because when he was sixteen—he was twenty-four now—he had gotten caught with three other fellows in a car they had borrowed just to go for a ride, and that was where he had learned to do some mechanical work. It was where he had gotten the Zig-Zag man tattoo with a straight pin and a Bic pen. The Zig-Zag man was the trademark on a brand of rolling paper.

The night she took him up to her own place, he rolled two marijuana cigarettes, and she smoked one, and then they "got it on," which was what Kirk called making love, and it was terrific, the first time she ever got so far into it that afterward she could not remember what had happened, only that she had been rocked and sweaty and exhausted and turned this way and that. His body was hard and lean, all strain and muscle, and his strong hands on her here and there knew just what to touch for how long and exactly how hard to press. She let him spend the night. It was strange to lie beside a man, strange but nice, and sometimes even after he was asleep she'd get the quakes and these little tingles, even though they'd stopped making love hours before. It made her smile, and she was amazed. While he slept, she rolled to her hip and touched his long, black hair, longer than her own, recalling how it had flared out about him, wild, as he had gripped her with his skinny arms. You could give yourself up to a man like that.

In the morning they made love again, but it wasn't as good because he'd awakened her and started right in, and all she could think about was that she had to pee.

A week later he moved in with her. It was sort of understood.

Kirk knew things, things you could not learn from a book, and Doralee Jackson respected that kind of knowledge. If you're hard up for a drink, you pour hair tonic through white bread, and to check you put a match to it. If it burned red, don't drink it; burned blue, it was okay. She couldn't believe anyone would be that hard up for a drink, but it was good to know a trick or two. He'd traveled a lot, and could tell her how to get from anyplace to anyplace else, reciting the interstate roads and where they came together or went apart, like the whole country was his backyard to play in. And she liked how sometimes they would go in a place and Kirk would get stared at for his hair, and he would stare right back, facing down the crackers, he called it, and she was glad to be stared at as the woman who was with him. Special. Different. She'd never known how much she needed that.

So when after two months of living with Kirk Dugan he said to her one day that he was ready to take off, her heart caught, but then she nearly wept when he asked if she wanted to go along. She did. She did, indeed.

He laughed at her when she said she needed a few days to settle things, especially to say good-bye to Momma and the boys. "That shit just holds you down," he said, but she insisted, and she felt even better about him when Kirk said it was all right, a day or two more would make no never mind.

Doralee was sure Momma didn't believe her story about a job she got in Denver, but Momma gave her fifty dollars and said to be sure to call if she got into trouble and needed more. She seemed tired, tired in a way that had nothing to do with working long hours. Lying to Momma didn't sit well with her, but she took the money. Daniel gave her a big hug and she promised to send him picture postcards of wherever she went, and as soon as she got settled they could all come visit her. And Jimmy listened to her talking to Momma, and then late that night while Momma was drifting off asleep in the big old living room chair, Jimmy took Doralee to the kitchen and while he drank a whole quart of milk straight from the carton told her that she must have thought their Momma was awful stupid. Doralee told him she loved this fellow, Kirk, and Jimmy nodded his head, wiping the milk mustache from his upper lip, understanding especially the part about how she needed to get out, there was nothing here for her anymore, never was, how she was sick of taking care of herself and just wanted a rest, and while Kirk Dugan wasn't some hero out of a book, he was not the villain, either. "If he treats you bad," her brother the all-state tackle said, "you let me know." He hugged her then, and that was all there was to good-byes.

So when Doralee Jackson got into the blue '78 Chevy Nova with Kirk Dugan way up in Iowa, she did not have many doubts, and if the truth was she did not have a pile of good reasons to go along, she did not have many reasons to stay behind. The doubts came quick enough, though, miles before they reached Mexico and the beach at Puerto Peñasco, but by then it was too late, she'd taken her chance, and she had to ride her play out.

The shower stall's blue tile was cracked and chipped from the floor to the ceiling, the grouting, brown and rotten, fell out in chunks, the double bed's springs squealed everytime you rolled over so that you woke up three, four times every night just from moving, and if you made love the damned thing made enough racket you expected every Mexican for two miles around to come by to peek through the raggedy cloth curtain that was nailed into the plaster and hung across the window that faced into the courtyard. The walls were a sickly yellow, the paint was peeling, and right above the bed was a hole you could see clear through to the beams, a hole that looked to Doralee like a horse, or maybe a camel. Over the beat-up bureau was a mirror, and beside that was a lamp with a three-way bulb that only worked at the lowest illumination.

But Doralee Jackson liked the room. And she liked that Kirk made slow love to her that first night, good as old times, and damn! how she liked that shower, rotten tiles, spiders, and all. The water was a miracle, hot as could be, so she came out with her skin tingling and when she pinched her hair she'd washed with the motel's soap, her hair squeaked and she felt her scalp breathe.

They took their meals in a small restaurant just outside the motel's gate, one of the dark luncheonettes they had wandered past that first morning. Eggs for breakfast and a hamburger at night. Doralee wanted to try shrimp Vera Cruzana, or shrimp in butter and garlic, but she kept her mouth shut because they had to pay cash in the restaurant. They were out of cigarette and beer money, so Kirk cursed up a storm and then pried off his boot heel and took out one of the hundred-dollar bills. Getting the heel back on he stomped around the room like a man gone crazy with roaches. It made Doralee laugh, and when Kirk first looked up at her he glared angry, but then he laughed, too. And the clerk in the motel office gave them change without batting an eyelash, but Kirk threw the deadbolt lock on the door that night and pulled the bureau to block the entrance, convinced they'd have their throats slashed while they slept.

Doralee might have wanted a bathing suit, but her cutoffs and a T-shirt worked okay. She might have wanted some tanning oil for the long afternoons on the beach, but she could do without, her skin naturally darker than Kirk's. All they did was sleep, swim, eat, make love, and sleep some more.

Four days in Rocky Point, and it was clear that no one was going to sell them dope. It would take Kirk a little longer to see that, or at least admit to what was already obvious. Well, it wasn't a bad vacation, and she'd be all right if he'd give it up and they would either head back to the border or to the south, maybe to a place called Mazatlán Doralee had seen on the map where they might have better luck. And if that didn't work, then Mexico City. Whatever it took.

The problem with men was you had to get them to think that everything was their own idea, and Kirk just didn't know how to admit he might have been wrong. He became cranky as a wet baby, hardly speaking to her at all.

Sometime after noon on the fourth day, the sun so hot and white a body couldn't even lie out on the beach, Doralee was in the room. Kirk was who knew where—probably asking dark-eyed little boys who had nothing to eat where the cocaine dealers were. An awful clanking came from the courtyard. She lifted a corner of the maroon curtain and saw a battered old bus pull up beside the Chevy. The bus was the kind that hauled kids to school, but it was grayish-blue, not a bright proper yellow. Mexico. Nothing was right in Mexico.

The men that got off the bus all wore open-necked sport shirts and slacks, bright reds and blues or yellows that were startling in Mexico where everything was sun-bleached to the same no-color washed-out dusty brown or gray. Each of them carried a duffel bag, and they laughed and cursed like men did when they liked each other and were having a good time. Mexicans. But there were three—the three who got off the bus last—taller than the others, paler, and no doubt about it, American boys. She saw them only a second, and then they walked toward the motel office, under the terrace in front of her door, and they were gone.

Later she was with Kirk out on the beach at a round concrete table that had an umbrella that probably once had been painted with colors but now was just metal-colored. They drank beer. The tide was out. All along the beach gulls and pelicans picked at whatever had been left by the tide along the rocky shore.

"You know what's wrong with Mexico?" Kirk asked. "You can't tell what's what. We were in the States, I would know what to do. Find a bar with a pool table, talk to a couple of people, and pretty soon we'd score and be gone. But fucking Mexico, man, fucking Mexico. I bet there's not a pool table in this town."

"Maybe we should head back."

"No way. We have to wait it out. They'll find us, soon enough. They'll find us. If I knew what was what, I'd find them, but I don't, so we'll wait."

"Maybe we should go south."

"South? What in fuck is south?"

"Other towns. Different people."

He chewed a thumbnail. "No. It'll be the same."

"You scared?" She stared out to sea, but felt his eyes on her.

"What's that supposed to mean?"

"Kirk, I'm bored. We're not *doing* anything."

"If you'd done time, you'd have learned patience."

"You did time?"

"Easy time. I told you. The boys' school."

"That's not like jail."

"Shows what you know. Juvey Hall could have been a fucking penitentiary."

She sipped her beer. In the south there'd be cool green jungles and blue parrots. What would that be like? You took a man from what he knew, he closed up. But she was unafraid to wonder. A woman would wonder.

One of the three American men she'd seen come off the bus was emerging through the archway of the cinder-block wall that divided the motel from the beach, trudging across the sand. He carried a towel, and he wore a proper bathing suit. He started going down to the water where some other people were clustered, people with children and coolers, fold-up chairs and fruit, but Doralee saw him notice her and Kirk, and he changed direction, easy as you please, coming toward them across the sand, taking confident strides with his long muscled legs, his bare feet sinking in the white sand, his straw-yellow hair falling over his eyes, a white country-boy smile big as the sky on his face. She kept her head tilted way back and her eyes open, the beer still cold enough in her throat, though she lost a bit that flowed over her chin and dripped to her T-shirt. She wished to God she had a bathing suit.

"Hi," he said, standing just outside the puddle of shade cast by the metal umbrella. "You folks are Americans."

"That's right," Kirk said.

"It's hot."

"Sure is," Kirk said.

"Why don't you sit down in the shade?" Doralee said, and Kirk looked at her sideways, his eyes squinted, but she made as though she was Dumb Dora and did not see him glance at her.

"Thanks, I think I will." He sat between them, closer to Dora than to Kirk, but not so close you had to think anything of it. "I'm Bobby

Kelly." He held out his big hand to Kirk, the back of his hand all covered with fine white hairs, the knuckles big and red, rough hands that had known work.

Kirk hesitated, then took Bobby Kelly's hand. "I'm Kirk Dugan. This here is Doralee."

"Doralee Jackson."

"Pleased."

Bobby Kelly was smiling at her, so hard she had to smile back. He was soft-spoken, and his voice had something in it she did not recognize, not Southern or Eastern, but something else that was maybe sorrow and made a girl want to take him home and keep him safe.

"You folks on vacation?" Bobby Kelly asked.

"Yupper."

"Staying at the old Hacienda, huh?" He laughed at some private joke.

Doralee had said nothing since she'd asked him to sit and told Bobby Kelly her whole name, and she knew that if she spoke she risked Kirk's anger later on, but to hell with him. Four days. He didn't know how to make things happen.

"I'm from Iowa," she said.

"Is that right? I've got a cousin in Iowa. In Davenport."

"I know Davenport."

Kirk sniffed as he wiped his lips after draining the last of his beer and throwing the brown bottle onto the sand.

"I'm from Oregon."

"You on vacation?" Kirk asked.

"No." Bobby Kelly swung his legs around and under the table, settling in. He put his elbows on the table. He kept right on looking hard at Doralee while he spoke, and she kept right on looking hard back at him. It was a contest. "I throw for the Penguins."

"What are the Penguins?" Doralee asked.

"The Puerto Peñasco Penguins. Triple-A Mexican baseball club."

Kirk laughed, a mean little laugh that made Doralee want to reach over and slap his face and pull his ears, but instead she said, "How long you been doing that?"

"Three years. I played for the University of Oregon and then came down here. I thought it might be a way to the bigs." His smile was almost an apology. "You know, American baseball."

Kirk took Doralee's still half-full bottle from her and helped himself to a long swallow. "How the hell can you play for a Mexican baseball team?"

"They allow four gringos to a team. I write home about the Penguins, and my Daddy laughs, says it isn't a decent name for a baseball team, sounds like we all wear tuxedoes and waddle in the outfield. But it's not bad ball, actually. Valenzuela once pitched in a league like this."

Doralee wondered who in Creation Valenzuela was, but she just nodded her head, trying not to smile because her teeth were so crooked, and she wondered just how windblown and ugly her hair might be. This beautiful boy from Oregon who wrote letters home to his Daddy— imagine such a thing!—this boy looked like he drank milk at every meal and breathed easy in the mornings.

She said, "Sounds like fun."

"Well, I wouldn't go that far. It's not much fun anymore. I just want to play a while, and I can do that here. Came down for one season, and here I am in my third. The money isn't great, but I get to play."

"If there's no money in it, it's bullshit."

"Kirk, don't be such a downer."

"Shut up."

"I'll say what I please."

"You usually do."

"Hey, I'm sorry . . . ," Bobby Kelly began.

"No problem," Kirk said.

They were silent a minute, watching the ocean, listening to the crash of the waves.

"I don't get to see many American girls down here. Thought I'd come over to talk a few minutes. Practice is at four o'clock and I've got just enough time for a quick dip." He smiled that big good-old-boy smile that made Doralee think of home. "You two are married, right?"

Kirk whooped, his head back and his long hair flying. Bobby Kelly's hair was short, longest in front.

"No, we're not married," she said, and added softly when she was sure Kirk was laughing so hard he wouldn't hear, "We're just traveling together."

"I see," he said and then smiled even more broadly at her, not leering, but glad, Kirk so busy laughing a gut-buster that he couldn't notice, and for the first time Doralee wondered how Bobby Kelly would become her ticket out of here.

Kirk wiped his eyes when he stopped laughing. "I used to play baseball myself," Kirk said. "Second base."

"That right?"

"Sure. In Illinois. At this school I was at for two years. Batted four-twenty-two."

"Is that right?" Bobby Kelly said, and smiled even wider before he pursed his lips and nodded like a man that knew a secret. "Heavy hitter like you would probably like to come to the game tonight. Eight o'clock. I'm pitching. Get you two seats right behind our dugout. Freebies."

Doralee said, "Yes," before Kirk could say a word.

Bobby Kelly smiled and said that he had to be off, shook both their hands—his hand really was rough, but nice—and headed right back for the motel without taking his swim.

"What the hell did you ask that cracker to sit here for?"

"Why not?" Doralee said. "I thought maybe he'd know somebody who might sell dope," she tried, knowing just from having looked at Bobby Kelly that he would never in a million years know anybody like that. But Kirk chewed on that notion a second. She watched his eyes cloud and then get clear. So she added, "And he probably speaks Mexican."

Kirk said, "That asshole probably doesn't know shit."

"Maybe he does."

"Maybe." Kirk threw an empty bottle at a gull that fluttered up and then landed right back, undisturbed.

"So we'll go to the game?"

Kirk drummed his fingers on the table. He looked out to the ocean where the wind made whitecaps on the waves, so strong it brushed foam into the air. "Sure. Why not? We'll have to find out where the damn ballpark is."

"We can find out."

"I hate guys like that."

"Guys like what?"

"Like that. Like that guy. So dumb. He thought I was married to you."

"You want to swim?"

"I want to fuck."

"I want to swim. First."

Kirk smiled, and as she stood he reached to pat her ass.

The tide was coming in and even though it was hot as could be the wind made her feel cool. She walked out a bit, stepping carefully on the rocks ready to hurt you, so unlike Iowa lakefronts where soft bottom mud sucked at your feet, and she bent to splash herself with the water, cold and smelling of salt, and then as a wave came at her she jumped straight up and when she came down she let herself sink, bending her knees, pinching her nose closed. Beneath the surface she opened her eyes and saw motes of light glowing from the sun, bubbles rising around her, and she listened to the total silence, so abruptly different from above the surface, and then she heard a roaring which was her own blood in her ears. She stayed under as long as she could, then exploded up, straightening her legs.

On the concrete terrace before the room Kirk said, "You swim like a shit."

"I never learned to swim."

"Well, you swim like a shit."

" 'Bout as good as you play baseball."

"What in fuck does that mean?"

But she didn't have to answer because they were going into the room and on the floor they found a little white envelope with two tickets and on the envelope in pencil was a map to the ballpark. Kirk picked it up and threw the envelope on the bureau. "Are you going to take a shower again?" he said and from behind her put his hands on her hips, pulling her toward him.

In fact, she wanted to. But she had figured out she would have to spread her legs enough to keep him happy, he was too damned dangerously close to being unhappy. She wanted him to want to go south with her, score the dope, make the money, buy the good life, have the good times, but Kirk could never be that bold. He was a mean, petty little crud. But there was no way she could piss him off if she wanted to go to that baseball game. She knew diddley-shit about baseball, had never

once in her whole life seen a game except on television, but now she
wanted to see a baseball game more than anything. Bobby Kelly might
be her chance.

It pissed her off. Kirk Dugan or Bobby Kelly. How did Doralee
Jackson's life become a matter of this man or that? Damn! She'd
fucked up this time.

She pulled Kirk's hands from her hips under her wet shirt and onto
her breasts and leaned back against him.

"I know just what you like," he whispered in her ear, "I know you
better than you know yourself, woman."

Doralee Jackson was still in love with Kirk Dugan the day they left Des
Moines, heading east because he wanted to show her Illinois where he
had been raised. But in the car Kirk became silent, and before they got
as far as Iowa City he all of a sudden twisted the wheel, bumped the
Chevy over the grass divider of the interstate so hard her teeth rattled in
her head, and told her that it would be better if they headed west. She
loved him for that, the quickness of it, the unthinking swift willingness
to allow events to take a course, and she was sure that afternoon that
she was onto a good thing because even as her jaw snapped together
when the car bounced over the divider she thought of the men she had
known who knew nothing of horizons and could never have done anything with less than a month to think, weighing chances and judging
prospects, until they'd bled the joy from it, thinking a thing to death.
So she was sure she was along for a good ride.

They went to Omaha where Kirk knew some people, and they stayed
there in a small apartment above a hardware store on the east side near
the Missouri River for a few days with Lee Harkin, a woman named
Sherry Anne, and their six cats. Lee and Sherry Anne would be out
during the day, so Doralee and Kirk had the place to themselves, to
make love on the sofa with the cats looking on, the sunlight strong in
the windows, with Kirk so cocky that he left the window shades up,
which embarrassed her some until she saw it excited her, too. In the
evening they would all smoke a little dope and then walk in the Old
Town or down along the riverfront, the gray river clogged with rusted
barges and cranes taller than the office buildings against the western
sky.

She liked Sherry Anne all right—she was a washed-out blonde woman older than herself who must have been pretty once—but Lee Harkin frightened her a little. A big man going bald, he had small eyes and a lot of dark hair on his arms. Kirk and he did some business, and Kirk told her later he had expected to do more, but that never happened. One night Kirk argued with Lee Harkin—she didn't know what about—and the next day they were in the car so early in the morning she was half-asleep, and all that day the car took them across Nebraska to Denver, Kirk not saying a word, just smoking one Marlboro after another, the Chevy filling with blue smoke, until late in the afternoon when the Rocky Mountains in front of them were like a wall that meant you couldn't go no further, Kirk punched the seat and said that Lee Harkin was a chicken-shit son-of-a-bitch mother-fucking asshole who'd lost whatever balls he might have ever had.

They didn't stay long in Denver, just a night and a day, and they slept in the car to save some money, something Doralee didn't mind a whole lot because Kirk was smart enough first thing in the morning to get to a roadside restaurant with a bathroom and what was a pretty good breakfast of eggs and home fries. He said he'd been in Denver lots of times, but he got lost on the highways until he finally found Larimer Square. He was sweet that day, standing by her as they walked in and out of the fine stores and she made believe she could afford the dresses and makeup, even in one place trying on this frilly red skirt with a white lace border that actually cost more than three hundred dollars. Another man might have gotten bored and antsy, but Kirk admired the clothes along with her, patient as could be, sitting in a chair near the try-on room sort of staring up at the ceiling and buffing his fingernails against his jeans.

They left Denver near four o'clock in the afternoon, and Doralee was all turned around, but they must have been heading south and east, because by eight o'clock they were in Kansas, and that was when Kirk pulled into the darkest part of a Stuckey's parking lot and told her to wait in the car, he'd be just a minute. Then he smashed the Chevy's interior light before he opened the car door, and with the motor running and the door left wide, he walked to where she could see him in the store's bright glare. He was carrying something heavy and black in his right hand just behind his leg. He came back five minutes later, and even by the dim green and amber glow of the dashboard she could see the heat in his eyes and the sweat on his face. He threw a brown paper bag at her, slammed shut the door, and the Chevy hugged the darkness back out onto the road half a mile before he put the headlights on, pumping the accelerator the whole time.

"You should have told me," she said when they were finally out on the highway and he was watching the speedometer, making sure he stayed right on 55. "You didn't have no right to assume."

"Honest, Doralee, I'd have told you except I was afraid you'd disapprove and leave me. I couldn't stand that."

Put that way, it was hard to argue with him, and she thought that maybe Hell was loving a thief.

She said, "It's dangerous."

"What's the difference? We need money. This is easy."

"Where'd you get the gun?" It was on the seat between them, big and black, and when she asked the question Kirk moved it under the seat between his legs. He took a beer from the back seat, steered with his knee while he popped the Bud.

"Lee. That pussy wouldn't do no work, but he sold me the gun. Two hundred dollars."

"I don't like guns."

"You expect me to go into a place and ask them sweet as pie to give me what's in the register? And they'll do it, of course, 'cause I'm so pretty, right?"

"I don't like guns."

"You just count what's in that bag, hear?"

Two hundred and twenty-eight dollars. More than she was able to save in three months when she had worked at two jobs in Iowa. She told him.

He smiled, drained the last of the beer, and said, "I figured it right, then. End of the day, dark enough that no one can eyeball the car, and the register's got the day's receipts in it. Pretty slick."

She kept her mouth shut. They did need money—you couldn't go anyplace without it—and when they made it to Wichita late that night, Kirk took her to the finest motel room she had ever imagined. Drapery on the windows, a terrace, real glasses, big gold towels, free movies on the color TV, satin border on the blanket, and plastic wrapped across the toilet so you were sure it was clean.

They walked across the road to a restaurant with table cloths and hot rolls in a basket covered by a napkin. After dinner, the night cool and the stars all out, she realized that she didn't mind much at all what Kirk did as long as he did it so no one got hurt. If that made her a thief at heart and as guilty as he was, well, she would sure be stupid not to enjoy the fruits of his labor. But he should have told her, and she knew she wouldn't trust him anymore, couldn't, because he was sure to get them into all sorts of shit sooner or later. The first sign of trouble—and it had to come, you couldn't just walk into anyplace you wanted wherever you wanted and take money without sometime, someplace having the roof fall in—the first sign, she'd be saying fare thee well.

She loved Kirk Dugan, right enough, but that wasn't the same as saying she was ready to give over her life to him, neither. Look at that sweet girl Sherry Anne. What did she have to show for her life with a thief except six cats in an Omaha apartment over a hardware store?

They drifted south and east a while. It got so that when Kirk told her it was time to stop someplace and make a withdrawal she got only a teensy nervous, sitting outside in the car, watching moths, expecting any second to hear the gun go off. But Kirk was a lucky man—she began to realize that, and like Momma had said, better lucky than smart—and not once did the slightest thing go wrong.

A hundred and thirty-seven from a Missouri gas station, seventy-eight from a convenience store outside Tulsa. They'd sailed down the Will Rogers Turnpike and Doralee watched out the window at the country passing her by, and she was sad for her Momma who'd heard of all these places but would never get to see a one, and here she was, Doralee Jackson from Des Moines, going places. It was not bad. When they had a room she felt clean, and she was happy to wash her clothes and Kirk's in the motel sinks.

Whenever Kirk Dugan stole, that night they lived high, and he would come at her those nights like a bull in breeding season, two, three, and once four times, and afterward he would lie across her exhausted, sweaty, and she would hold him, her fingers laced in his damp hair, and she wondered at the mysterious workings of men, one day cold and so far in themselves you thought they'd forgot your name, and another so filled with force it took her breath away, and how that had to have something to do with what they'd done and how strong they believed they were, but had nothing to do at all with how they felt for a woman.

Driving west in Oklahoma, Interstate 40, Kirk pulled over into a rest area because the sun was in his eyes.

"Why don't you drive?"

"I don't know how."

He thought that was so damned funny, but this was a day he was most like the sweet boy who'd leaned over the seat of a white flatbed truck and followed her all the way to a bus stop, and so he right then and there decided he would teach her, there was so little to it.

They both laughed the two times the car stalled, and then he had her drive in circles and then in figure eights until she learned how much she had to press the brake and how much to turn the wheel, and then Kirk said to her, "You ready for the highway?"

"No way."

"Sure you are."

"Kirk, I can't do that with all those trucks and such."

"Nothing to it. You just keep her at fifty-five, point her, and go."

So he talked her into it, and she stayed in the right lane.

The tires drifted onto the shoulder once, and she raised dust, but he just leaned toward her and almost daintily touched the wheel until they were straight on the road again. Then he said, "You've got to do more than forty."

She was too scared and worried just with going straight to look at the dashboard, so she near wet her pants when he sidled next to her and with his left boot pushed down on her foot and the car speeded up.

"Stop that!"

"You just steer."

"Goddam it, Kirk. Goddam it."

But the car went faster and faster, and Doralee was in a sweat. He would get them both killed for sure, but pretty soon she liked the feel of it, how the car, a ton of machinery, responded to the slightest move she made on the wheel, or the brake, or the accelerator. She drove all the way to Weatherford, and they stopped there. It was something to know she could drive a car if she had to.

That night they were in this beer and pinball machine bar and Doralee was sitting beside Kirk on a high stool, getting more than a little cockeyed giddy on the beer and juke-box country music. He suddenly said to her, "Sit tight. I'll be right back."

She thought he was going to the men's room, and he did, but when he came back he was wild-eyed and she knew he had done something.

"Let's go, Doralee," he said and took her elbow.

"I want to finish this beer."

"Let's go sweetheart I mean right *now!*"

He practically lifted her off the stool, and they went straight out to the car, drove right by the pretty motel where they had taken a room, and out onto the highway. That was how Mr. William Krantz lost his wallet and credit card, taking a leak in a Weatherford bar they called a private club because Oklahoma was a dry state. So private you joined at the door and then drank as much as anybody else.

He showed her what he'd gotten, and explained that the credit card might do them good for two weeks.

"What did you do to get it?"

"I just took it."

"You hit him?"

"Not much."

"Damn it, Kirk. This is different."

"How's it different? I swear, I didn't hurt him much. He'll be fine. What in hell you worried about? Hey, I walked in and stood behind this guy until he got his pecker out and started to pee. You should have seen his face when I reach out and took his wallet. He must have thought he had some queer fiddling with his ass. He spins around, still pissing on the floor, and before he opens his mouth I hit him one good one in the belly. It was pretty funny."

He charged a tank of gas, and she watched carefully to see how it was done, having never owned a credit card. That Kirk Dugan certainly knew things.

They slept that night in the car beside the road, just over the Texas border. As she listened to Kirk breathing in the front seat and she lay curled up in the back, able to look up through the rear window at the stars over Texas, she knew that he was changing. Or she was. Whichever, it didn't matter. She was not so stupid that she believed he only

had to hit that man once. No sir. William Krantz must have taken a few
hard shots, and Kirk Dugan, the sweet boy who'd leaned across a truck
seat not giving a damn about traffic while he talked to her, that Kirk
Dugan had given them to him. She hadn't thought it was in him.
Maybe it was that exact moment—it was hard to tell—but maybe it was
that moment she became more wary of Kirk Dugan than in love with
him.

The tedious long roads of the Southwest were like nothing she'd ever
seen. Mile after mile of oil rigs and sky. The ride made Kirk talkative,
and she found out then his real name was Alex, Alexander Wilshire
Dugan, and that he'd "borrowed" cars as a boy in Illinois and spent
two years in juvenile hall where he'd met Lee Harkin and a bunch of
others he talked about, most of whom he'd lost track of, but he was
sure they were doing fine. She had her doubts but kept her mouth shut,
gazing out the windows at cattle pens and railroad tracks and the flat
land, endless flat land that ran forever brown and away. They saw a sign
that said 150 miles to Amarillo, and they both could not believe they
were still that far from anyplace—when did Texas end?—so when Kirk
said they could kill time and drive all at once, she didn't even think
much about what he suggested but unzipped his fly and went down on
him right there in the car, in broad daylight at sixty miles an hour. It
seemed sinful, she was hot and bored, but she took no pleasure pleas-
ing him, and so she was sure she was out of love with Kirk Dugan.

He told her she was a good girl, and that he wanted to do right by
her.

The very next day, headed west into New Mexico after a dull night in
Amarillo, he told her he had this idea about running dope up from
south of the border to Los Angeles, and that way they'd make a lot of
money fast, and maybe they could stay put for a month or two, live
high, and have a hell of a time. His eyes got bright and he slapped at
the wheel, all excited about what he started to call his plan.

"What will we do with the money?"

"Damn, Doralee, you ask the dumbest questions."

"Well, you answer that one for me, then."

"Why, woman, we'll live it up."

"Like how?"

"We're talking about big money here. Maybe a few thousand dollars. Shit, can't you think of what you would do with a few thousand dollars?"

"I want to know what you'd do."

"We'll get a nice room someplace. Eat good food. Maybe buy some clothes. How's that? Sure. We'll go right back to Denver and get you that red skirt. How'd you like that?"

"I'd like that fine. But I still don't know just what you want to do with so much money."

"Aw, shit. *Spend* it."

She'd wanted to hear him say something else. Anything else. But there he was with no imagination. And hell, she couldn't think of a damned thing, neither. What *did* people do with money? Maybe settle someplace, buy a business, a little card shop or something, and she caught herself, right then, it was a revelation, here she was thinking about not being on the move, just like the men she'd known back in Iowa that she'd thought were so damned lame with their heads and asses buried so deep in black Iowa dirt they'd never think to move. It was a revelation that she, Doralee Jackson, wanted a place that was hers and something to do there. Yes, it was Doralee that was changing, faster than Kirk Dugan might or probably ever could. They said that travel helped a person find herself. Well, she'd been traveling, and it had been one kick-ass journey, but already it was getting old. All Kirk Dugan was was lucky, and no one's luck held out forever, but she couldn't very well say to him, No thanks, drop me off here.

They'd been on the road three weeks.

When Bobby Kelly reared back, foot higher than his shoulder, and threw the ball, the ball sliced through the air and hit the catcher's mitt with a sound that let you know that ball had been *thrown*. Chunk! Doralee swore that it sizzled, hissing like the zipper on a winter coat as the ball traveled to the catcher and then Chunk!

You could see every bit of Bobby Kelly in that ball, him falling forward following his arm that had windmilled over his head, all that power right down to the fingers. How the catcher didn't get knocked on his ass was a wonder. It was special to be sitting right behind the dugout watching Bobby Kelly warm up right there on the third base line, sitting in Bobby Kelly's seats.

The top of the dugout gritty with dust was painted a pale turquoise. Kirk Dugan sat way back in his wooden seat beside her, his boots pressed against the cyclone fence trying to make like he wasn't impressed.

They'd found the ballpark easily enough, had parked on a dirt field surrounding the place where everyone left their cars every which way so it was clear no one could leave until everyone left together. This was Mexico, and the common sense of a lined parking lot just could never occur to no greaser, Kirk said, what could you expect?

You would not have thought there were that many people in all of Puerto Peñasco, men smoking cigars and swilling beer from bottles, women with babies in their arms, and what must have been a million children running loose. The field was no pretty patch of emerald grass like on television, but was scrubby and dusty in the infield, and nearly all dirt and pebbles in the outfield. There were no stands out there, just a scoreboard and a big old fence painted with advertisements in Mexican—mostly for beer but one for Coca-Cola—and there were big lights on tall posts that lit the place like day. Moths fluttered at the lights, moths so big you could hear them pattering into the glass, and the night was warm and sticky, the air thick with the smell of grease and fried peppers.

They played some music on the PA system, everyone stood up, and then Bobby Kelly and the rest of the team came out from the dugout, right out from under their feet, and before they started to loosen up and throw the ball around Bobby Kelly came over to the fence and said he was real glad Doralee and Kirk could make it, and when he smiled that American-boy smile so filled with perfect teeth Doralee couldn't help herself but had to smile right back, her crooked teeth and all. A fellow carried stuff up and down the aisles, and Bobby Kelly shouted in Mexican—which proved she was right, he could speak the lingo. The next thing she knew, she and Kirk each had in their hands a paper cone of ice and syrup. Raspberry for her and orange for Kirk. Cold and sweet, coating her throat, delicious. Kirk tried to give the guy some pesos for the treats, but he wouldn't take any, and Kirk bitched about that. Then Bobby Kelly said he had to go to work and he started to throw, and that was when Doralee got so impressed with the sound of a baseball.

Hissss-chunk!

"Look at these greasers," Kirk said. "They're so short no one's got a strike zone."

"What's a strike zone?"

"Boy, you are dumb," Kirk said, but not disrespectful, and he started explaining about knees and armpits, but Doralee was watching the men on the field who looked downright snappy in their uniforms, pinstripes on white flannel, blue lettering, and little caps, and she liked especially how the pants fit. Bobby Kelly had a great butt, and she wondered how she hadn't noticed that on the beach that afternoon, but she remembered it was his hands she was looking at then.

"Do you think he's any good?"

"We'll find out in a minute, I suppose."

"This is fun, Kirk."

He snorted. "Better than the motel room. Why don't they have any television in Mexico?"

She knew barely enough about baseball to follow what was going on, but once the game started she was pretty sure Bobby Kelly was doing all right. The first player he faced struck out, and the next two hit little dribbling shots that were picked up easily and thrown to first base. The Penguins trotted in and she could hear them chattering in the dugout.

"I thought he'd talk to us," she said.

"Nah. Pitcher's got to concentrate."

"He's doing good."

"He's doing all right. When I was a pitcher, I used to do all right."

"I thought you played second base."

"That, too. I played lots of sports. Basketball. Football."

Her brother played football and she knew what her brother and his friends looked like, so she just looked at skinny Kirk Dugan whose real name was Alex and she didn't say a word. He couldn't even bullshit in a straight line.

There wasn't too much excitement, it seemed to her, as the innings went on. Just once a Penguin walked to first base, and that was all that happened. Kirk leaned forward, intent on the game, and Doralee wondered just what her Momma would think of her girl now, sitting in the hot sticky night beside a robber, Doralee, a friend of the pitcher for a Mexican baseball team. She was a long ways from home, she was.

"I tell you, they are throwing smoke," Kirk said. "That Bobby Kelly has a cannon in his sleeve."

What was smoke? "Well, I guess, but I wish something exciting would happen."

"Doralee, you are dumb as rocks, I swear. We've got us two no-hitters going and you want excitement."

"I knew that." She licked her fingers where the ices had melted.

Then Bobby Kelly was standing with the bat in his hands, and he let two pitches go by, but on the third he swung and *craaaack* hit the ball a good one. She stood automatically, just like everyone else, it wasn't something you thought to do, and her fingers gripped the fence. "Go, go!" she heard Kirk yell. The ball sailed high up, past the lights, and then came down right into the center fielder's glove, right at the fence. There was a big sigh from the seats, like everyone let go their breath at the same time. Bobby Kelly was already to second base and he slapped his cap against his leg with disappointment, but came right on in to get his glove and start in pitching again just as though nothing had happened and he hadn't almost hit himself a homerun.

Bobby Kelly threw and nobody hit the ball past the infield. Twice the ball was hit sharp right at him, but both times he sweet as you please caught the ball and gently tossed it to the first baseman. People clapped. By God, she was friends with a star! Then one of the American fellows on the other team cracked the ball a good one down on the ground, and it looked as easy as the others had been, but before it got to the shortstop it hit one of the pebbles and bounced over the fellow's head into the outfield. The seventh inning, and he was the first man to get to first base. The noise was like to make you deaf.

"That wasn't good, huh?" she said.

"I'd say, Doralee. Bad luck, but that shithead should have got the ball anyway."

"You think?"

"Sure. You need reflexes good as mine to play this game."

Bobby Kelly seemed different then. He walked around the pitcher's mound a few times, his face grim, and he picked dirt out of the bottom of his shoe. He dug a little hole with his toe, walked around a few times more, stood with his hands on his hips and looked to the outfield and the darkness beyond the fence, like he was talking to God or something, waiting for an explanation, while all the time a new batter was waiting for him to get started. Then he turned and tried to seem ready, but Doralee knew he wasn't.

He kept glancing over his shoulder at the fellow on first. That fellow had Bobby Kelly's chin on a string and was giving it a tug. Twice Bobby Kelly threw to the first baseman, but there wasn't any heart in it. He threw to the batter, and it should have been a strike, and there was a hell of a groan from all the people in the stands while Bobby Kelly stood and stared at the umpire like the umpire was in on some dirty secret, the same secret that had made the ball hit a rock and sail into the outfield. But he pitched again, and this time the throw was so high the catcher had to jump up to keep the ball from getting past him. The catcher walked the ball back to Bobby Kelly, taking his time before returning to home plate. Sweat shined on Bobby Kelly's face, and he kept wiping his brow with the sleeve of his shirt, tossing the ball into his glove three, four, five, six times before a pitch. The fellow on first would run a bit to second, then scramble right back, and you could see that Bobby Kelly was going to lose it. When Bobby Kelly threw, Doralee couldn't hear any hiss on the ball.

He pitched one that hit the dirt and bounced past the catcher, and the runner hustled himself to second base, got there standing up and just grinned at Bobby Kelly. The greasers booed, but that didn't seem fair to Doralee, because while Bobby Kelly might be in trouble, it was no fault of his.

"Can he do that? Just run to second like that?"

"He sure can. I tell you, that boy is in deep shit now."

And on the very next pitch the batter hit one way, way out to a spot no one could reach. A double. They put a 1 on the scoreboard.

The manager came out, stood a while talking to Bobby Kelly, and then Bobby Kelly walked slowly in, kicking dust, his glove hanging from his hand, his head low.

She'd have thought he was angry or at least sad, but just before he walked down the steps to the dugout he looked up at her and the damndest thing! He winked at her. He winked!

The Penguins lost. 3-0.

It was only a minute or two back to La Hacienda. Kirk left her in the room while he went out to hunt up a six-pack of Mexican brew. "That Carta Blanca shit ain't half bad," he said. Doralee stood on the terrace in the hot night and saw the team bus roll into the courtyard. She'd have thought the players would be down, but they were laughing and noisy as if they'd won. She tried to pick out Bobby Kelly but couldn't because it was so dark, so she waited a bit, then went into the room to take a shower. Just as she was pulling her shirt over her head, there was a knock on the door—not like Kirk who never knocked—and she knew it was Bobby Kelly.

Dressed in regular clothes again, a red golf shirt with an alligator on it, he was with two other fellows, also Americans, also baseball players, and damn! they were handsome. Nice boys with pressed pants and neat little thin black belts around their waists. She wished to God she had some clothes besides jeans and T-shirts, but they didn't seem to mind at all, big grins on their faces, big bare arms coming out of their short sleeves down to their big wrists and hands.

"By Heaven, Bobby, you were right. That *is* an American girl," one of them said, and you could tell he meant nothing mean by it from the way he said it, and the three of them laughed. Doralee found herself laughing too, standing in the doorway of the room, glad for the dark so they could not see that she blushed.

"Where's your hippie friend?" Bobby Kelly asked, and before she could answer turned to the other fellows and added, "I swear, this guy has a ponytail."

"Naah. Nobody but assholes wears a ponytail anymore."

And she looked, and looked again, because it was the fellow from the other team that had hit the ball, gone to first, and given Bobby Kelly all that trouble, and here they were, together, and they were friends. How could that be?

That was when they all heard Kirk Dugan's boots coming up the walk, and they heard him say from the darkness before they could see him, "What's going on?"

They were delighted to see Kirk had some beer, because they had some, too, along with some tequila down in one of the rooms, and since they were having a party just for gringos would he and his lady friend like to join them?

Doralee said, "Sure we would," before Kirk could say a word—she wasn't about to let this chance pass her by—and that was how they wound up downstairs in a white-walled room with red curtains that must have been Bobby Kelly's place when the team was in Puerto Peñasco.

Kirk whispered to her, "What the hell are we doing this for?" as they'd gone down the stairs, but he settled in once one of the baseball players rolled a monster joint, big as a cigar, and in a few minutes the place was foggy with the sweet smell of dope. They had a big ghetto-blaster with tapes of American rock 'n' roll music, and Doralee realized just how much she missed home. All the Chevy had was an AM radio that once they made it to Mexico got nothing but static or Mexican stations that played nothing worth hearing. Bobby Kelly's tapes were mellow, college-boy music, and when Kirk asked if he had any country-western Bobby Kelly gave him a mournful smile as if to say he expected that from him and was sorry to have his expectations come true.

They tossed themselves about the room, on the bed or on the floor, a sweated cold beer in each person's hand, passing a bottle of Cuervo they either tilted straight up and gulped or poured a little into their beers. And the joint passed around the room, and then another. Pretty soon Doralee had herself a buzz and the tequila was making her sweat, but it was damned nice to hear American voices other than Kirk's again. Nice boys. Nice American boys.

Rick Johnson who'd gotten a hit off Bobby Kelly was from Wisconsin. He said that if Bobby Kelly had gotten some hitting from his team, there was no way they'd have beaten him and it was a shame he had to pitch for a team that gave him no help, and how in hell the scorer called that shot he himself had gotten a hit was a mystery to him. Best man on Rick Johnson's team, Rick Johnson said, was the Penguins' groundskeeper that couldn't rake off a damn rock. He said to Kirk, "You wouldn't score that a hit, would you?"

And Kirk brightened up and said, "I thought it was an error."

Stan Foley who also pitched but hadn't that night was from Maryland. He said, "No way. It was a clean hit, Kirk."

And Kirk had to say, "Maybe."

So Doralee could see what was what. They were putting Kirk in the middle, but in a way he'd never know it, baiting him, making him feel like a fool without knowing why, and Doralee figured that out because she was watching Bobby Kelly's big grin get wider and wider. These boys were so free and easy, it was a wonder. Liking each other, liking what they did, telling stories about where they came from and what they hoped to do. They drank beer and rolled another joint, and Bobby Kelly popped the tape on the box and put in another, mostly Bob Seger and the Silver Bullet Band, hot music that made the room hotter and Doralee could feel the sweat trickling down her back, making her T-shirt stick between her shoulder blades. She sat cross-legged, a bottle of beer on the floor next to her, and she was grinning as broad as Bobby Kelly.

Kirk told a story about how he once put a Cadillac engine in a Dodge, going into detail about just how it was done, and when he was finished Stan Foley looked him in the eye and said, "Why in fuck would anybody *want* to do that?" and the baseball players right away started talking about fly-fishing, Rick Johnson saying there was no place like a Wisconsin lake. Doralee saw Bobby Kelly punch Stan Foley in the leg when Stan Foley cut Kirk so short, and she saw that Kirk didn't see.

Bobby Kelly went to the bathroom and when he came back he sat on the floor between Doralee and Kirk, so she could hardly see Kirk at all.

"Do you dance?" he asked her, and she said she didn't.

The baseball players groaned at that, all saying of course she did, nice like, but she was just shy being the only girl at the party, wouldn't she try? She said she didn't know how, and Bobby Kelly said that he would teach her.

So they stood up, and Doralee Jackson from Des Moines, Iowa, who had never danced before, danced. "Just move with it," Bobby Kelly said, and the tequila, the marijuana, and the beer made it easy. She was swaying at first, and they all clapped when she gave a bump with her hips—Bob Seger screaming about that old-time rock and roll. She bumped it again, raised her hands over her head, closed her eyes, and felt the sweat pop over her face, down her neck, on her chest and belly, her skin feeling like it was alive and creeping, and when she opened her eyes all she saw was Bobby Kelly. This was dancing. They were moving like they were one person. The song ended, and Rick Johnson up and gave her a whirl, and then she was dancing with Rick Johnson and Stan Foley at the same time, and she felt like a queen, these big handsome American boys giving her all this attention. The song ended, and she had to sit down to catch her breath, and she noticed Kirk still on the floor with his eyes clouded black and mean, his lips thin and tight, and she suspected she would catch all sorts of shit later, but she refused to care. They were in Mexico where nothing made sense, least of all Kirk Dugan's big plans, and by God she would at least have a little fun.

Maybe Stan Foley had seen what Doralee had seen in Kirk's face, because when Doralee sat down he asked, "What are you folks doing down here, anyway?"

While Kirk answered him, Bobby Kelly's hand found Doralee's sweated knee, patting it in time to the music, and she did not push his hand away. Kirk said, "Business. We're here on business."

That got the baseball players laughing again. Bobby Kelly asked what kind of business could anyone have in shitty Puerto Peñasco? "If Mexcio had an armpit, we'd be breathing Right Guard."

"I got business," Kirk said. "I got business. And maybe you boys can help."

Stan Foley smiled and popped another beer. "How's that?"

"I want to score some grass, man."

"He wants to score some grass, man."

"The man says he wants to score some grass. How much you talking about?" Stan Foley said.

"Bulk. A couple of bricks."

"You're talking weight, huh?"

"That's right."

Doralee could see Bobby Kelly was holding in a laugh, and Rick Johnson was rolling on the bed like he was having a fit, but Kirk was so hungry after what he wanted he couldn't notice anything else.

Stan Foley went on. "How much money you got?"

"Enough."

"Well, shit, I don't know anything about that stuff."

Rick Johnson guffawed into a pillow when Kirk muttered "Bullshit," and flicked a bottle cap across the linoleum floor.

"Tell me," Stan Foley said, "Where'd you get the ink?"

Kirk's hand went to his tattoo. "This here? I got that in a jailhouse."
He said it slow for the effect, to show he was tough, but the baseball
players kept grinning and looked at each other.

"I tell you what," Stan Foley said. "You come out with me for a walk
to my car and maybe we'll talk a little business."

Kirk's little eyes narrowed even more, the temptation eating at him,
and then you could see he yielded to it. "All right. But don't bullshit
me."

"Have I ever lied to you?"

Stan Foley stood up, and with some effort, Kirk did, too. They went
out into the night. A few minutes went by and Rick Johnson said he left
something in his room, he'd be right back, and off he went.

Now Doralee was not so stupid that she didn't know what was going
on, but the funny part was that Kirk did not. So she said to Bobby
Kelly, "Does that fellow really sell dope?"

"No. Fact is, Stan got this marijuana from his sister when she was
down here two weeks ago to visit. No problem passing customs going
south. We don't fuck with the stuff much. Hell, we work here. Mexican jail is bad news."

She smiled, shaking her head still buzzing from Cuervo and music,
her body still perspiring from dancing, like the beer itself was pushing
out through her skin. It made her bold. "Well, are you going to kiss me
or not?"

Bobby Kelly put his big warm hands around her waist and pulled her
toward him. She opened her mouth and he opened his, their saliva and
sweat making the kiss slippery, and her head spun with it, his hands so
good on her, her leaning toward him, his hands moving on her belly
and up under her shirt, a long slow kiss that took her breath away, but
she was worried that Kirk might come back any second now, so she
stopped him.

"What are you doing with that hippie asshole, anyway?"

"I don't know. I just don't know."

He kissed her again, this time teasing his tongue all along her upper
lip before she parted her lips and his tongue explored inside her mouth.
This was so good, so good. Her pants were getting wet. She kissed him
back, hard, urgently, and he asked her if she wanted to do it right then

and she would have said yes, taken him right there on the floor, this big old American baseball pitcher from Oregon, but she said, "Kirk might come in. Later?"

And Bobby Kelly just smiled that big American smile. She didn't know if she meant it. It was something to think about, it was.

He went to the ghetto-blaster and turned over the tape, which had run out while they were kissing, and right then Stan Foley and Kirk and Rick Johnson came back in, so with her and Bobby Kelly at opposite sides of the room they looked as innocent as kids at a church picnic. Kirk was still scowling, but he looked puzzled. Stan Foley must have gone on with the lie, telling Kirk what he had to to keep him interested, but not enough to let Kirk believe he had found his deal. It would be easy to fool Kirk.

They partied. Drank more beer, smoked more dope, chased the beer with tequila—the second bottle, now. Bobby Kelly had had his taste, and now with the half-promise of "later" was staying far away from her. What would it be like to have Bobby Kelly?

Nice, but it would not happen. She watched that man in his red golf shirt and pressed pants that weren't so pressed anymore, and she suddenly hated his easy confidence. He must have planned getting into her pants since the moment he saw her on the beach, thinking she'd be easy, and for sure eager to tell his buddies all about it later. And yes, she had played along, but she saw in an instant it was time to call a halt, time for Doralee Jackson to take control just like she'd always done. She should be able to handle a little tequila, a little beer, and a little desperation without giving herself to some bright-smiling Bobby Kelly. A girl had to break bad habits before they had a chance to take hold.

But Kirk Dugan wasn't for her, neither. No sir. She could do a lot better than that. She could dance now—there was nothing to it, you just up and let yourself go—and Kirk Dugan was so dumb he couldn't see past the nose on his face or think about anytime more than next week. She felt sad for him. He was getting sloppy and loud, talking how he had done this and had done that, that these guys didn't know shit until they stepped in it.

"Aww, hippie. Cut it off," Rick Johnson said.

"Who're you calling a hippie, motherfucker?"

Rick Johnson got the giggles. "What kind of ponytail is that?"

Kirk touched his head. "You fuckers think you're so smart."

"I am too tired for this," Rick Johnson said, and without another word got up and left the room.

"Asshole," Kirk muttered.

"I think he's got a point," Bobby Kelly said, and when he said it Doralee sat up straight and took a deep breath. Here it was.

"What point is that?"

"That asshole ponytail, friend. That's bush league. Coming down to Mexico without knowing what you're doing, that's bush league. All that jailhouse shit, that's bush league. All talk."

"I'll tell you what's bush league. Playing baseball in this shithole. That's bush league."

"Hey, man," Stan Foley said. "It's baseball. What's better than playing baseball?"

"That's right," Bobby Kelly said, placing a beer to his lips.

"Lots of things. I do anything you guys can do with my eyes closed."

"Whee-hew!"

"You laughing? You laughing at me?"

Bobby Kelly nodded. "Why don't you name something?"

"Fighting."

Stan Foley laughed. "He's got you there, Bobby."

Bobby Kelly just smiled that big smile and glanced at Doralee. But she didn't smile back. It had felt good to kiss him and it had felt good to have his hands on her, but what he was about now made her less than human, some damned reward, a blue ribbon at the fair. Bobby Kelly wanted her not because of who she was, but as the sign that he had in some way gotten over Kirk Dugan.

"Tell you what, hippie boy. Fighting is out. I got to be on the bus tomorrow night and I wouldn't want to break my hand on your jaw. . . ."

"That's a pussy excuse if I ever heard one."

"But I'll take you on in anything else you want to try. Fair and square. Doralee here can be the judge."

Kirk looked at her. She looked right back. He was wondering. Well, let him wonder.

Kirk said, "You think I don't know what's what? I know what's what."

Bobby Kelly said, "You swim?"

"He swims great," Doralee said quick as she could, and Kirk looked at her suspiciously, then puffed up some. "Oh, Kirk tells me he's a fine swimmer." So she got him in, gave the push and nailed shut the door, and now she'd see how it would work.

Bobby Kelly said, "Stan, you remember our swimming contest?"

"I do."

"What we'll do, hippie boy, is swim out in the ocean next to each other, nice and easy like. Just right next to each other. And the first one to turn back is the loser. Nothing to it. No race. Just to see who's got the balls. You want to try that?"

Kirk looked at Doralee for a second, sipped his beer, and said softly, "You're on."

"Well, that's fine," Bobby Kelly said, and he gave his hand to Kirk to help him up. "Stan, you coming down to the beach with us?"

"You bet," Stan Foley said, but as soon as the four of them were out in the night heading for the concrete wall that separated La Hacienda from the broad crescent of sand, Stan Foley lost his legs, sat right down on the blacktop of the courtyard and said, "Boys, I do believe I am drunk."

They all thought that was pretty funny, but they couldn't get Stan Foley to stand, tugging on his arm but him falling back on his ass, and so they left him there, a beer bottle in his hand, and just before they passed under the arch Kirk turned and yelled, "You remember we got business tomorrow. You hear?" and they heard Stan Foley shout, "Yessir. Big business tomorrow," and he cackled with laughter.

Doralee walked between Kirk Dugan and Bobby Kelly, both of them with their arms around her waist like the three of them were old friends, the men's hips bumping hers, the sand sucking at her feet. She thought how stupid men were, trying to prove something that needed no proving, and she knew that they were going at it because somehow or other they believed she had agreed to be the prize.

She didn't like that, and she didn't care for either of them thinking that she was some damned trophy, so she kept her mouth shut, saying to herself, let the damned fools do what they will. Doralee Jackson was done going along for rides just to see where she'd end up.

They got to the shoreline and Kirk threw his beer bottle into the black water.

"We just swim out and back?"

"You got it, hippie. First one to turn around is the asshole."

"Then I got no problem," Kirk said.

Doralee sat down on a small hill of sand, cold and damp in the dark. It must have been four or five o'clock in the morning. The clear air had burned the alcohol from her blood. She was sober. The breeze at her back chilled her, drying the perspiration from her T-shirt, and she drew her knees to her chest and locked her arms around her legs to make herself tight and warm. Gooseflesh rippled on her arms.

The moon was setting, shining just the slightest crescent of silver light, a hand's width above the black water smooth as an Iowa lake. By the color-bleeding moon she saw the two men undress, not saying a word now. They sat to slip off their shoes, then stood, and she heard the ghostly jingle of keys as they stepped from their pants and then took off their shirts. In the moon's light it was hard to tell one naked man from the other, the light reflected off the water making them two silhouettes, Kirk the more wiry of the two, but otherwise completely the same. Kirk's black hair was no different from Bobby Kelly's blond in the moon's light. Two American boys who had somehow arrived at this Mexican beach. She heard them say a few words, though she could not hear what, and then the two shapes walked beside each other down to the water lapping at the shore, and there was greenish sparkle about their ankles as they walked forward. She could still see them black against the silver streak of moonlight reflected on the surface when they were waist deep, and then she lost sight of them, but she heard the gentle sigh of a splash as they began to swim away from the shore, and she thought maybe she could see flashes of phosphorescence as they swam, and then she couldn't even see that, just the darkness of the Mexican night and the flat smooth glassy black surface of the sea.

She rubbed her hands against her bare arms trying to stay warm, and she wondered where the birds went to at night. Pelicans and gulls, did they make nests? or bob around on the sea waiting for morning? A fistful of cold sand trickled through her fingers. The moon slowly sank beneath the water and the breeze at her back picked up, and then after a time behind her the sky turned pink and she watched her long shadow that went down right to the waterline get shorter. She peered out over the water and saw nothing, as she expected, felt the warming sun on her, and stood to see further, but she knew there was nothing out there anymore for her to see.

To her left was the pile of clothes. They were damp from the night air. She took the keys to the Chevy from Kirk's jeans and with the keys pried the heel off his left boot. Two hundred-dollar bills, neatly folded. She could drive the Chevy good enough, she thought, and she'd have that long drive north over the Mexican desert to get better at it. Or south. Why not? How could she get lost? There was just the one road and she would go anyplace she pleased, do anything she desired. She'd survive, and if she found the right place, she would do better than that. It would not be easy, but nothing worth doing ever was.

She thought of the credit card, but decided there was no point in asking for more troubles. She would have enough. She wondered how the waves breaking on the shore—crashing in, flowing out, crashing in again—could sound so sorrowful and lonesome. A gull fluttered to the surface of the sea and floated lightly on the undulating surface, and she thought how she was the only person in the world who would ever know that beneath a white rock with a scratch on it in the Arizona desert a gun lay hidden, and that chances were that gun would rest undisturbed forever and forever.

Marmosets

This fellow Paul, I knew, lived for several years with a woman and eight marmosets. An anthropologist, as an experiment the woman took in a pair of the animals and treated them as members of the family. The whole bunch of them lived in Paul's place. Marmosets being what they are, little monkeys, after a time there were eight of them, and anthropologists being what they are, eventually off she went to some university in the Pacific Northwest. The marmosets went to a few zoos; the two originals, Rebecca and Tony, to the zoo near Paul in Arizona. I learned this from Paul when we became friends; from the anthropologist I never knew.

Some of us feel compelled to work, but Paul was spared this affliction. At his father's death he inherited a small house and enough money that the interest bought groceries, so long as he never ate steak. A cautious man, he never touched the principal. Also he had a Navy pension, having taken seven ounces of shrapnel in his calf, an accident while on maneuvers in the South Pacific in the late '60s. The injury was not bad, but Paul walked with a slight limp on the final nine holes of a round of golf. You would guess he fatigued easily, but that was part of his game. He golfed in the low eighties and enjoyed playing for a few dollars, and when you saw him limping you were tempted to wager a dollar more. Limp and all, suddenly his drives soared fifty yards further down the fairway's center, and his putts became deadly, as though the ball had grown eyes. With a bet, his low eighties became middle seventies.

I met Paul at the time in my life when my marriage was finally collapsing. I'd just lost my third business. My father, may he rest in peace, a year or so before he died said to me, "Promise me one thing, Ira. Never go into retail." We were playing pinochle. He pulled at his ear lobe and did not look up from his cards. I promised, but then I met the woman who became my wife, and she believed that the only way to success in America was that a man work for himself. "No one on salary ever became rich," she said. In bed she would read to me from a book she had about Colonel Sanders and Henry Ford.

First there was a shoe store in a shopping mall, but it dropped dead when everyone went crazy for athletic shoes. You don't want to know from the greeting card store we bought after that, but I learned there are only three rules to the retail business: location, location, and location. The vacuum cleaner repair place under the el we bought in Brooklyn, that was a terrific deal. The guy was retiring, and he himself floated us the loan to take the place over. A leveraged buy-out. A little gold mine. What could go wrong? Only two problems: I can't tell one end of a wrench from the other, and I discover my right hand has maybe three thumbs.

So before we left the East with four lawsuits pending against us, I went out to the cemetery in Queens and visited my father. It's nice there, green and the air smells fresh. "Abe," I said, "you knew from what you were talking. It's a shame I didn't listen."

Three kids, the wife, thank God no dog, we drive to the Sunbelt. Everybody was doing it. We look around Tucson, and my wife and I agree the best chance is to open one of those computer game arcades in a storefront.

To change a place is not to change a life.

Two years after coming to the desert we are waiting for a monthly check from my in-laws, my kids are eating tacos and beans, and one day my wife figures out there is no reason for her father the hero and her mother the virgin to support their gorgeous grandchildren, their brilliant daughter, and their son-in-law the schmuck, too. Something has to go. The schmuck is asked to leave. I can see my kids whenever I want, but that was no bargain. My wife would give away ice in the winter, as my kids I would not wish on a P.L.O. terrorist.

I was hanging on, hoping I could find a buyer for the business. I would have taken half of what I put in, even 35 percent, and would have been glad to get it. I could stall the guys who rented the machines, I thought, for another month. Pay them I would never be able to do.

One afternoon I am in the store, and this kid, playing hooky for sure, with a single lousy quarter for half an hour is blasting spaceships. A regular Luke Skywalker. I decide I want to play golf, just to get to a place that is quiet and green for a while, and so I pull the plug on the kid. Like I have ripped out his heart, he screams. Only 4,000 from his all-time personal record! Never *ever* will him and both his friends spend their quarters in my machines! If his two cockamamie friends show up, I will make another fifty cents, and this, I explain to him, is not so much that I will prepare to retire. I throw the little cossack out, lock the place up, take myself to the municipal golf course, and this is when I meet Paul. We are sent out as a pair.

You may think it funny that I like golf, but what's not to like? I'd developed a taste for the game the two years I was in college. Walking relaxes a man. What's prettier than a well-tended green?

I confess, when I first met him, I thought maybe he had a few dollars, and if I could talk right, sell it right, he would lend me some, but as we went around I saw that wasn't the way it was. On a shoestring he lived, really. We stopped at the nineteenth hole, and over the beers he bought I mention I can't live without trying to work at one thing or another, and he explains that all he can see in that is forty or fifty years of drudgery, and then with luck playing golf whenever he wanted, and here he was at thirty-four years of age doing that already, so why not cut out all the misery in the middle? He played tennis, too, he told me, and since I did not, we agreed to meet the following week on the golf course.

Well, I didn't get to sell the business. One morning I show up and find a marshall sealed the place tighter than a Presbyterian's lip. Since I am used to eating and do not like to sleep in the park, I look around and am lucky to find a sales job in a men's shoe store. Experience I got. It was nice to have a regular check coming in for the first time in my life, and I am overjoyed to let someone else have the headaches. Best of all, I don't start until two in the afternoon, which means my mornings are for golf. My wife would have sneered at my being a wage slave, but I didn't care what she thought, as that week I am also served with divorce papers. I pick up my kids one afternoon, just because I miss them more than I thought I could, and there is a lot of talk about "Uncle" Jimmy who owns two ice cream parlors, so I know the score.

It made me sad. My first lesson in what is really important. You lose an investment, you lose an investment. You lose your family, what's left?

I was thirty-nine, as low as I'd ever been, and I admit it looked to me like Paul had the world by the short hairs. Ambition takes a man only to grief.

During the next few months I learn that except for two years at sea Paul is always a student. Sometimes he used a word or two I never heard before, and sometimes he talked about things I could not understand why anyone in their right mind should care. Who ever got rich from reading Irish poets? He'd never married, though he'd had three "serious relationships." Children he don't know from. I tell him he is missing what it is all about, and he asks which of us has known more grief. It is hard to argue with a smart man, especially when you are worried he is right.

A handsome man. From athletics, he was muscled as a greyhound. From the outdoors, he was tanned as a movie star. Hair was on his head, shaggy, brown, and all his. He never looked his age, more like twenty-seven, so when he starts in on me to go with him to chase girls, I am amazed. I look in the mirror, I see a frog, but Paul tells me that I am just out of practice. I'd watch Paul with his dates, and I saw he was a gentle man, soft-spoken, a man who listens. He had a way of bending his head that let you know he cared about everything you thought or said, and he did not want to miss any of it.

One night we go to the movies with two lovely women, we go for drinks, and then we drop each of them off. Paul always likes to end an evening with coffee at Mo's Deli, not so much because Mo's coffee is so good, but because at Mo's you are served a basket of these tiny sweet rolls that are baked with so much butter your heart surgeon would jump for joy. The relish tray is a work of art. Pickles like that out of New York I never saw.

No matter what time of day you go to Mo's, there is a line to get in. In fact, three lines, because to make the service quick Mo has these chrome chutes at the door. One chute for couples, one for parties of three and four, and the third chute for larger parties. I admire the business smarts that makes such an arrangement. In the restaurant business, after location, everything is turnover.

In the tourist season they always put a boy out front to explain the three lines to people. All he had to do was ask how many are in a party, and then direct people to the proper line. The boy's name was Billy. Paul always says hello to the kid, and if there is time they talk sports.

That night is not time. It is tourist season, the late movie rush shows up, and there must be a convention in town, because I never saw so many people at the door of Mo's. Maybe there were rumors Mo loses his mind and is giving away cheesecake. It is a nice night, though, and no one seems to mind standing on the sidewalk outside the restaurant, except Billy.

Billy rushes into the place, then comes out, slapping his forehead when he sees even more people, then he rushes in again, then out. Frantic. When he stands still, he bounces on his feet like a kid who's just thrown a baseball through a window and doesn't know which way to run. He was all over sweat. Paul and I said hello.

"I can't stop to talk, fellas," Billy said. "I never seen so many hungry people."

Billy had that kind of open, simple smile that let you know right away there is not much upstairs. If Billy had been sixty-seven years old, you'd still call him a boy. Maybe, in a way, he is lucky. In fact, Billy was twenty. His straw-blonde hair fell over his forehead. His clothes never fit right.

When God makes His mistakes, it is our chance to be kind.

We watch the kid work. As I said, it was a nice night, but he was hot. Off comes the yellow blazer they make him wear, and a few minutes later gone is the black bow tie. He leans his head through the door and shouts over a customer, "What's going on in here? Let's snap it up. I got hungry people that got to get in. I got hungry people out here."

Paul calls him over and puts his hand on Billy's shoulder. The kid keeps looking back to the restaurant to see what is going on. He can't stop bouncing on his toes. The lines get longer. Paul tells him to take it easy.

"I can't. I can't. There's too many people here. Too many," he says and off he goes.

Paul says to me he thinks Billy is in a bad way and that someone should do something about it. I agree, but what was there to do? I think of my kids, who, all right, are not terrific company, but thank God I can look on them and not feel pity. With kids it is like anything else. You take your chances, do what you can do, and accept the bad with the good. More people come. Billy tries to get the people into three lines out into the parking lot, but there are no chrome chutes out there, and there is no way to keep people in the neat lines he wanted. He starts to get crazy, telling people that they are dumb, feeding people is an important job, and if they would just stop being stupid and listen to him they would get in and get fed much faster.

It goes on like that for maybe half an hour, and then four elderly people who've moved past the front doors are discovered to be in the wrong line, the line for parties of five and more. They sidestep a few people and exit from the wrong chute in order to get to the right one, and when they do, Billy puts his hands on this old cocker and pushes him. Thank God, he did not fall. A hip on such a man shatters like glass.

"You see, stupid!" Billy screams, his face right up to the man's, spit flying from his lips. "You didn't listen to me. You didn't listen. Now it's all screwed up. All screwed up. Stupid old man!"

They left, of course. All of us on line were uneasy. We came for pastry and coffee, and we were seeing something not pretty to watch. Paul is nervous. He says to me maybe we could go someplace else, just to relieve the crush and maybe help Billy out that way, but I said no, it wouldn't make any difference, who can hide from troubles?

Mo himself comes out. Mo was a short, round, balding man who was probably born with a cigar in his mouth. No one, not even his mother, has ever seen the cigar lit. His shoes are polished, and he walks like a penguin, with his feet pointing out. Mo comes from the store and asks Billy what the hell is going on.

Billy starts to cry. "I'm sorry, Mr. Mo," he says. "There're too many people. There are too many people. They're hungry people. I'm trying to do like you said, but there's just too many hungry people."

The kid's legs fold like he is screwing into the earth, and he sits on the pavement. He pulls at his hair.

Paul had to turn away. I did not.

Mo goes into his restaurant and comes out a few seconds later with some money in his big hand. He picks Billy up by the collar, like you would a kitten, and pushes the money into the kid's pocket. "Get a cab," Mo says not ungently, his words sliding around his cigar. "Go home, Billy. Rest up."

"What about all these people? It's an important. . . ."

"I'll take care of them," Mo says. He pats Billy's back. "We'll see you tomorrow." The kid wiped his face on his shirt sleeve.

A bit later, Paul and I drank our coffee. We sat at the counter, just to speed things up. Paul dips a butterhorn into his cup.

"Golf next Thursday?" he suddenly says.

"Sure," I say. "You can beat my pants off."

"Poor Billy."

"'Poor Billy'? What 'poor Billy'? I'm sorry for the kid, but someone has to run the elevators, no?"

This is what I have always believed. Everyone tries. You do the best you can. After that, it's God's will.

"I was thinking how he has to expose himself to situations that he can't deal with. All the time. Everything he sees is overwhelming. You understand?"

"No."

"I mean, if you play your cards right, if you're careful, you never have to take a chance. You and I, we can do that. But Billy can't."

"Maybe you can," I said. "Me? I have to make a living. The first thing you learn in business is that the risk has a lot to do with the return."

He bit the pastry. Then, as if startled by his own sloppiness, he stabbed his index finger at the crumbs that had fallen to the countertop.

"I could have gone with her," he says. "I could have taken a chance."

"Who?"

"Her name was Margaret. Did I tell you that? Margaret."

"The one with the monkeys?"

"Marmosets, Ira. They were marmosets. Never call a marmoset a monkey. He'll get hostile."

"What chance?"

He shook his head. "It's strange. Like that kid, Billy. He's limited. Locked up. I'm locked up. Just the same."

I said, "No, it's not. Billy hasn't got the tools."

Tilting his head back, he drained his coffee. I could see the muscles in his throat working. I doubt he heard me.

We played golf that week, and right after that Paul disappeared. I tell you, I felt deserted, betrayed, but why not? What did he have to keep him around? Who did he have to ask permission from?

Six months go by. I kept the job, and pretty soon they make me the manager, and with that comes a raise. I will never be rich, but I will never wonder where my next meal comes from. I met a lady, and I adored her, and for a reason God alone knows, she adored me. We were planning to be married. She wants kids, and I am amazed to discover that so do I. How else does a man leave his mark?

One day the telephone rings, and it is Paul. Did I want to play a round of golf?

We met Thursday morning. His game hadn't changed; he beat my brains out, and even took five dollars of my money. I was glad to lose it to him. I'd missed him.

His tan had faded, though he looked healthy, and his hair was cut shorter than he had worn it when I'd last seen him. After the eighteenth, we headed for the clubhouse for our beer.

I wasn't going to ask, and he wasn't going to tell me. I am sure I could have asked, but it seemed indelicate, as though I would be prying into a place in a human heart where I had no rights. Who can tell the longings that pull at another man? I do not know for certain where he had gone, though I could certainly guess, and that he was back could only mean that some risk had brought no return, some hope had borne no fruit. Believe me, I know all about hope denied, more than I ever care to know again. I admit, I was curious to know what went wrong, and so I told him about my fiancée as much to share with him my good news as to oblige him in some way to tell me about himself.

He looks at me as though I were strange. "Things are really better?"

he asks, and without waiting for an answer he says, "Well, how do you like that?"

Instead of telling me his news, after we swallow the last of our second round, Paul asks me if I have a few minutes, he wants me to meet some old friends. I did not have the time, but because of the way he asks, how he pulls at his lip, I could not refuse.

I was surprised when instead of to his car, we walk from the club-house to the street, down a block, and into the city park next to the golf course. The park is filled with mothers and their children, retired men and women, a few young lovers, all sitting around the lake. It is early afternoon, and the sun is high and hot.

Paul walks without saying a word, and I follow him. He walks by the lake, past the candy stand, directly to the zoo. He pays the attendant for my admission as well as his own. He walks more quickly now, his limp pronounced, turning to me just once to say, "You want to see this, Ira."

And then we are near the primate cages. He goes straight to them, Tony and Rebecca, the original marmosets that he and the anthropologist had raised as their own. They must have smelled him before they saw him, because as we come around a bend there is an awful racket, and when they see him, they screech and their long hands curl out from between the bars to him, the fingers spread, their little bodies pressed against the bars and wiring. They cling to the bars of the cage with their feet and tails, pulling so hard that the lock rattles, and they chatter enough to make you deaf.

Paul leans against the restraining banister and slowly raises his open hand, palm up, his fingers spread. Shrieking, the marmosets reach. I see Paul hesitate, and then he abruptly drops his arm. He won't let either of the two creatures touch him.

"My family," he says to me. He turns back to them and makes some soothing noises, but they do not calm down. They keep reaching for his hand, but he will not lift his arm. "That's my family," he says.

Steering Clear

Aaron Pendergrast could smile big as a pumpkin, and he smiled most of the time. He was a happy man, and how many people can you say that about? His friends paid no heed to the whispers that Jamie was just too perky and quick to be the product of any union between Grete and Aaron. What difference? Jamie was ten, and Aaron had been beside Grete since Jamie's birth. If that's not enough for some people to qualify a man to be a father, then some people maybe have to rethink what's important. We understand what's important hereabouts. We liked Aaron Pendergrast. We knew him.

Grete had blonde hair and a figure that made a man glance away and think how he'd settled for not enough. She laughed easily, and it made you feel good to be near her when she laughed. A comer with a Denver surveying company, she'd quit our high school when she was a senior cheerleader to marry Aaron just before Jamie was born. You wanted somebody to make your office run better than a hundred-dollar watch, you wanted Grete. She made no decisions, but she sure enough ran the place, and to their credit her bosses knew it. After seven years they gave her a small piece of the outfit just to make sure she wouldn't think of moving on. Now and then the work took her north to Laramie or Cheyenne, or south as far off as Santa Fe or even Phoenix.

One afternoon at Moira's Coffee Shoppe fellow name of Claude Richey was feeling mean. Eight months before, Richey's old lady, Lucille, had wandered off for six weeks. She'd come back sudden as she left, suitcase in her hand. Under the kitchen table light where he'd drunk a lot of lonesome beer and he'd fed their three kids stacks of

pancakes, all he knew to cook, Richey likely thought of the hell he
wanted to give her, but he couldn't do it. Took her back without a
word. Took her back for fear she'd leave again.

Richey said to Aaron, "You don't worry about your wife when she's
away?"

Aaron scooped Moira's apple pie into his mouth. All that sweetness
pleased him, and that pumpkin smile broke across his face.

"You don't know a damn thing about wimmen, Aaron, you know
that?"

Aaron scratched his head. He really thought about it, grinned, and
said, "You know, I doubt that I do."

But Richey was a dog with a rag doll in its teeth. "Don't you ever
think about it? Don't it ever worry you in the night?"

Aaron wiped his lip, scratched his jaw, and said he didn't see how
Grete might do anything in Laramie for three days that she couldn't do
during lunch in Denver. "No point in worrying what you can't help,"
he said and drank his milk.

"Damn fool."

We told Richey to shut up, the man had answered his question, and
Richey shook his head in sorry disbelief or maybe what was envy.

Past few years, Aaron has had his own business. Reliable Shuttle.
Grete set that up. Aaron humped a van from town to the Denver airport
carting businessmen. Snow, ice, wind, Aaron Pendergrast picked up
and delivered. Never had an accident. Stayed on the right and steered
clear of trouble.

As far as Aaron was concerned, the best thing about his work was it
gave him time with Jamie. He was home all midday. Grete was a natural woman, but busy, so Aaron had pretty much raised the kid, cook-
ing, cleaning, going to the PTA and the like. We called him a
housewife, and he'd laugh and say, "That's about right, boys, and I
love it." You can't get the goat of a happy man by reminding him just
what he is happiest about.

Ten, Jamie was old enough to know a world bigger than her backyard. Hormones still asleep, she wasn't prone to the craziness that
takes us all at thirteen or thereabouts. She'd tear through the streets
coming home from school on her bicycle, a pretty pink thing her
Daddy had painted and polished, black hair swirling around her,

candy-red color in her cheeks like her mother's, legs pumping, her mouth open in a laugh. Jamie had no special toys, the best stereo, or some such, but the pack of girls she traveled with just naturally went to the Pendergrast place to do their homework, giggle about boys, sprawl on the carpet and be silly while experimenting with lip gloss and nail polish. Aaron being there most of the time, you see, the house was safe, comfortable, and the truth of it was that a father will indulge his little girl and her friends where a mother will feel it is important to prepare them for the grief and hard times to come.

So many kids popped in and out of the Pendergrast place, it was difficult to pick any one out, but Aaron noticed Enid. There was her name, and these days when every female child has a name that ends with "a" or is named for a flower, just having a basic handle like "Enid" is a distinction. She never gushed or shrieked, but Enid took in the world through her heavy pink-tinted glasses like a judge contemplating a repeating felon. Leaner, taller, baby-fat gone, not yet a woman, she was just a straw-blonde stick of a girl with pale pursed lips, hollow cheeks, and a way of talking that Aaron guessed meant her people were from maybe the Deep South. Enid didn't say much, but when she spoke the other girls took what she said as final. "Wouldn't it be wonderful to know Michael J. Fox?" one of them would moon, and the others would giggle or sigh with that faint prepubescent longing that doesn't yet know its own source. But then Enid might say, "He's really older than he looks, you know. Probably not that much fun," and the other girls became subdued.

One early spring afternoon the Reliable Shuttle dropped its last passenger at the Best Western and Aaron headed home. Aaron was whistling, and maybe as the rest of us will do when he got out of the van in his driveway he paused a moment and looked up to the Rockies in the west. You can live here all your life and see the Rockies every day, but the man whose soul isn't now and then lifted by the sight of the snow-covered mountains against a blue spring sky has no soul at all. He stepped around the pile of bicycles, up the three concrete stairs to the kitchen door, and into the house.

"Jamie?"

She didn't answer, but galloped up the stairs from the half-finished basement, bolted into the kitchen where her father already sat unlacing his boots at the table Grete insisted on calling the breakfast nook, and threw her arms about his neck. His child always smelled of shampoo, and when she played hard, as she had been doing downstairs, that odor mixed with the stale smell of perspiration at her scalp. He loved it. Lips smacked a kiss at his cheek, and he patted her bony behind as she ran back to the basement door. He noticed her hips were widening. The thoughts of a happy man eddied through his mind like mist. He ought to finish the tongue-and-groove pine paneling in the basement and maybe start planning a drop ceiling, he had put off trimming the edge of the kitchen door for too long, Grete wanted to plant a line of rose bushes in the backyard and he could surprise her with that before she came back from Laramie tomorrow, he ought to resurface the driveway because the freeze-and-thaw this winter past had done its work. These half-thoughts were the pleasant haze of responsibilities within which a happy man will live.

Jamie said from the door, "Can Enid stay for dinner?" and because she charged down the stairs before he could answer, he had to shout, "Sure, but call her mother first."

Aaron popped a beer and read from back to front the *Denver Post*. He was unaware of that big grin spreading across his face. One by one Jamie's friends left the house, each time the screen door shut banging like a gunshot.

Beer always made him feel nicely fuzzy. Spaghetti? Or a can of soup and let the two kids make sandwiches of cold cuts? He could let the children decide. That was easiest.

"Hello, Mr. Pendergrast."

What was it about the child? Wheels turned within wheels within wheels in that little head, he knew. Enid was somber, probably smart. The pink sweater she wore was too large for her, unraveling at the elbow. If she'd have extended her hand to shake, he'd not have been surprised, but she stood with her hands behind her back, a private at parade rest, her thick glasses magnifying her eyes.

"You call your mother yet? It's getting late."

"Whoops," his daughter giggled.

"I'll do that now," Enid said and nodded.

The two girls went to the telephone in the hallway just outside the kitchen. Aaron turned another page, found the business reports, and flipped past them. Jamie dialed the telephone, and he thought that odd. He heard her talking to Enid's mother—he supposed it was her mother—and he heard his daughter relaying the conversation to Enid. Well, kids were strange and would not always find the direct way. Her mother didn't know if she could stay. Call back in half an hour.

They returned to him. Jamie started to tell Aaron what he already knew and he waved a hand at her. "I heard," he said and glanced at the wall clock. How *much* should he prepare? The woman's indecision was an inconvenience, but not serious. What could be going on at Enid's house that a half an hour could make a difference? "You'll just have to call back."

"My mother is having trouble," Enid said.

"I'm sorry to hear that."

"All the time."

Aaron watched his daughter watch her friend. Jamie was puzzled. She asked the question Aaron had avoided.

"What kind of trouble?"

"Her boyfriend, Frank." Enid pulled at her sweater's unraveling thread. "She always has trouble with Frank. Can I have a cookie while we wait to call?"

"Help yourself. You know where they are," he said and smiled, but got no smile in return. Did Enid ever smile?

He watched her eat one Vienna Finger and jam three more into her jeans pocket where they had to be crushed to crumbs. The two kids went back to the living room. Finally at the paper's front end, Aaron tried making sense of the national news. The kids whispered, but Aaron could make no sense of what they said, either. Truth was, he didn't care to. He wished Grete were home. Grete was better at these things.

Jamie appeared at the door. "Can Enid sleep here tonight?"

"It's a school night."

"She can wear my clothes tomorrow and she has all of her books. Can she, Daddy?"

"Well, if her mother. . . ."

"Thanks, Dad."

Down in Denver, the paper reported, they were experiencing a crime wave. Assaults were up. Rapes. Burglaries. Murders were down,

though. He quickly turned the page and went again to the comics.
Garfield was tripping up Odie, and that dog always made him smile.

The two girls rejoined him, sat beside each other across the table in
the breakfast nook. Strong sunlight penetrating the curtain lace fired
the room, making Enid look more blonde and his own daughter look
more dark. They were a paired set, like those two magnetic Scotty dogs
that came in a cellophane envelope from a vending machine. Enid
squinted up at the clock, then elbowed his daughter, who burst into
speech.

"Enid's Dad doesn't live with them."

"Uh-huh." Aaron had to close the paper. He couldn't help himself
and had to ask, "Where is he?"

"Penitentiary," Enid said. "He didn't do it, but they say he did."

"What was that?"

"Embezzle. He's been there four years. Momma got the divorce two
years ago. I used to write to him."

"That's hard."

"Frank lives with my mother. They fight. He has two children, but
only Rachel lives with us. Rachel is sixteen. Rachel is why they fight."

The kid was perfectly controlled. She might have been reciting multi-
plication tables, except that she was crying. When Jamie cried at some
disappointment, all of her cried. Face all puffed, she'd gasp, nose
running, she'd make her racket, and in a few minutes it was done,
finished and forgot. But not this kid, no sir. It was eerie how Enid
cried. Only her eyes betrayed her. They went red, they brimmed, and
then like bad plumbing overflowed. Her motionless hands remained
folded on the table. Aaron patted her hands. He had to do something.
Enid nodded.

But Jamie was smiling. What could she know about real trouble? His
daughter was blessed with that naive faith possible for a happy child. It
was why she'd brought her friend in to him. He knew that. Why should
any kid have a life like Enid's? He wanted for his daughter's sake to say
something, be able to do something, but for that matter, what did
Aaron know about trouble? He knew only a bit more than Jamie knew,
and that was to steer clear.

"Maybe you should call now," he suggested.

Jamie went to the telephone. Enid's serious eyes so large in their frames held him.

"She wants to talk to Enid," Jamie returned to tell them.

Enid's shoulders sagged and her eyes reddened more as she hauled herself to the telephone.

Aaron sat a second, and then like the times you drove past an auto collision and even though you didn't want to you turned your head and looked, he followed them to the hallway. Enid's face was streaked. She sniffed. A shock of her blonde hair fell over her eyes that she pushed away. She held the receiver close to her face. His daughter was still all right, though. Something was happening, he could tell she knew that, but nothing could happen that was so bad Daddy couldn't fix it. Enid carefully replaced the receiver in its cradle.

"I have to go home. Can you drive me? My mother wants to talk to you."

"To me? What does she want to talk to me about?"

Enid shrugged. Her lower lip trembled. It was getting late. He would have to drive the kid, her bicycle in the back of the van. But he wouldn't talk to the woman. He would drop Enid off, wherever it was she lived, unload the bicycle, and he and Jamie would go straight home, fill the kitchen with the warm mist of boiling water and the aroma of spaghetti sauce. It would be all right.

Enid gave perfect directions, sending the van across the railroad tracks that ran straight north-south through the town. The two kids shared the front seat beside him. The Rockies cast their shadows over the plain. Enid wiped her nose on her sweater sleeve. At the limit of his vision he saw Jamie's face begin to crumble, her automatic certainty in the goodness of things diminished now that she was beyond the warmth and light of her father's kitchen. Grief was a contagion. Gripped by a nameless fear, Aaron jolted the van over the silent policeman of the apartment complex.

"Building D," Enid said.

They stopped on a roadside apron of brown dust. Quick as he was able, Aaron rushed around to the back of the van, but the woman must have been waiting at her door. Before he had a chance to wrestle Enid's bicycle from the van, she was beside him.

"I need her here tonight," Enid's mother said. "The son-of-a-bitch. I need Enid here. I'm outnumbered. You understand how it is? Come here, Enid. Stand by me, darling."

"We have to be getting back."

"That bastard." Her arm curled around Enid's neck and her thin hand rested on her daughter's narrow chest. "It's not him, though. It's not. If he'd talk to his kid, do something with the little slut, we'd be all right. Isn't that so, honey? Can I tell you what happened yesterday? I get home and right there on the living room floor the little whore is fucking this guy. Now is that right? Next thing she'll be bringing niggers into my house. And dope. There's dope, too. I can't say anything to her. I'm not her mother, thank God. It's not my place, is it? So today I had it out with him. I said to Frank his daughter was a whore and there was no way in God's creation I had to put up with this bullshit. You know what I'm talking about."

Jamie moved closer to him, pressed against his leg. He tried to smile. Enid's mother shifted her weight and pulled a crushed pack of cigarettes from her pocket. She lit one with the burning stub of another. The two ends of the cigarettes seemed to Aaron to kiss. The woman's neck was strained and taut, the skin tight.

"Enid could stay with us for a while if you. . . ."

"No. No. I need her here. She's my girl, you see. If her father wasn't so damned stupid I'd have what I need, but he was more stupid than a man needs to be and so Enid here is my only support. You understand these things, right? People like us know the score. It's just one damned thing after another. Shit. I just wanted to tell you so you wouldn't think I was some crazy woman or something. That bitch has got to move out. That's the long and short of it. The guy had a tattoo on his ass, I'm here to tell you. A fucking skull. Now, that's proof, isn't it? Ain't that proof?" She tapped her foot. "You're from around here, aren't you?" she said suddenly.

"All my life." His hand, he realized, was about his daughter in the identical way the woman's was about Enid. He wanted to shield his daughter's eyes as he'd done when she was little and was frightened by the witch in *The Wizard of Oz*, just for the moment hold the horror invisible.

"We have to get home."

He didn't wait to hear what she said but boosted Jamie up through the rear doors of the van and then banged the doors shut, pulling once at the handle to be sure the doors were locked. Then he brushed by the woman and her child, and though it was now dark he could see Enid's eyes on him, as though by some trick the lenses of her thick pink glasses were able still to hold a glint of light. He started the engine, and the woman was rapping on his window, hitting the glass with what must have once been her wedding ring, though now it was on her right hand.

The woman's lips formed the words "Thank you." Beside her Enid stared up at him. He was in a lifeboat, the child was in deep water.

He slammed the van into gear and the wheels spun, then caught. Aaron turned on the radio—he wanted sound—but Jamie turned it off. He looked at her. His daughter huddled small against the passenger door, her face reflecting the amber and green lights of the dashboard. As though she were cold she hugged her knees, and as the van jolted through the streets, her head bumped the glass of the window. She sucked her lower lip into her mouth.

"What is it?" Aaron said, hoping in some way his voice would help.

"It's so hard for her," Jamie said. "It's so hard. It's not fair."

He could think of nothing to say. When he reached to pat Jamie's leg, she shied away from him.

He fed Jamie the cold cuts. They ate in silence, and then watched some television the same way. Jamie was put to sleep at the usual time, and she clung a touch harder than usual to her father's neck when he bent to kiss her. He had to push her hands away. "Enough of that," he said and with his finger touched the soft black hair from over her eyes. As he closed the door to her room he wondered what he had meant.

Aaron rested alone in the living room. The day wouldn't sit right. The kid, that damned kid Enid, what had she done to deserve what she was getting? How was that possible? Jamie was calling to him. "Daddy." Again and again. "Daddy." He pretended he didn't hear. If he went to her, he did not know what he could say. Not knowing made him angry. Soon enough she was quiet, maybe asleep. And soon enough all of her would awaken.

He tried not to think, but he kept coming around back to that woman at dusk. She'd been so thin her jeans rode on her hips and you could see the line of her bones. She'd flicked the cigarette ash two, three, four times before she puffed on it, and she held the cigarette like a man, between her thumb and forefinger. *People like us.* What did that mean? He'd had to leave the kid there. There was nothing he could have done. Nothing at all. Damn! And there was nothing he could have said to Jamie. He knew no words. He drank a beer, hoping alcohol might dull the edge, return him to that comfortable mist of half-thought, but his mind remained too sharp, too focused. The kid's eyes had been so damned large! She could see too much. And what was he supposed to do? He was angry, dammit, angry. At what? At what?

Near ten o'clock he dialed the number of Grete's hotel in Laramie, his large fingers clumsy on the phone. Grete would know the right words, say the words he needed to hear that would let him see just how it was all right and there was nothing to worry about since there was nothing to do. She'd explain it to Jamie, also.

She didn't answer. He listened to the telephone ring twelve times.

"Are you sure you've got the right room?" he asked when the switchboard girl came back on the line.

There could be a thousand good reasons Grete wasn't in her room at that hour. Aaron thought of them all. He tried her again at 10:30. And again at 11:00. When he called at 11:45, Grete lifted the telephone.

"I need you," he said.

Grete laughed pleasantly. "Philip? Is that you?"

We understand what's important hereabouts. We liked Aaron Pendergrast. We knew him. He was a happy man. So we know why Aaron Pendergrast didn't miss a beat, but immediately shouted into the phone, "Grete? It's me. Aaron. This connection's bad. I can't hear you. I can't hear you at all."

What Doesn't Kill Me

What doesn't kill me makes me stronger.
—Lenin

"What was it like?" Maggie asked.

Lizabeth looked away. Sun, strong, clean and bright through the glass, superheated the porch. Tourists a week ago had loaded their station wagons and left them the beach, empty except for seabirds and a few die-hard sunbathers, like the sisters, residents of the island. Terns strutted in nervous community. Isolated sunbathers lay more solid than the dead. As a child, right after they'd moved here for the year 'round, this had been Lizabeth's favorite time. She'd been home almost a month.

"What was what like?"

"I don't know. Everything. Being married. Being divorced."

"I'm not divorced yet, Maggie."

Lizabeth's younger sister shrugged. "You know what I mean."

The wicker swing's chains softly creaked as Lizabeth's bare toes pushed at the warm linoleum. Maggie sat on the floor, her legs folded beneath her. A sharp line of shadow slashed across her chest. Her torso and bare legs were in stark light, her face in darkness. What was she, eighteen? She looked like Betty or Veronica, for God's sake. A sophomore. She would be returning to school in another week. Lizabeth tapped cigarette ash into the potted fern where four butts bent like hairpins were among the woodchips.

"It wasn't fun, Mag."

"I guessed that."

"Then why ask?"

"I just wondered. Sisters should talk. You're eight years older than I am, but I thought we should talk."

"Seven."

Maggie's eyes clouded, and for a second Lizabeth thought her sister would have to count on her fingers. "Eight at this time of the year. My birthday's not until October."

The smoke in her lungs burned, harsh. Mornings, she coughed. Her voice rasped until coffee. It didn't matter.

"You remember the summer I was fifteen? You were eight, I guess. You remember that summer? Every time Billy Anderson picked me up in his dune buggy, Mom said I had to take you with me. You remember?"

Maggie said she didn't remember.

"Disco. That was the summer of disco. Everywhere you went, disco music was on the radio. I hated you that summer. Mag, I'd have drowned you if I got half a chance." She sucked the final drag from the cigarette and decided to see how long she could wait before the nervous itch of need would make her light another.

Maggie's fingers traced circles on her calves.

Lizabeth said, "It was like that. Being married was like that."

Maggie's black hair and eyes glinted sunlight as she shifted herself closer to her sister. Her hand brushed hair from her eyes. "I meant the good parts. I want to hear about the good parts."

Lizabeth allowed the swing to come to rest. She didn't care for the sensation of being suspended, but none of the porch furniture suited her and the swing at least had height. There'd been good parts, of course, early on. In fact, mostly before. But marriage could ruin things. Since her sister was an airhead, she said, "There were no good parts."

Maggie was quiet, then said, "At least you didn't have children. That's something."

Lizabeth stared at her sister. Maggie's instincts were a mole's. She burrowed to what was crucial but lacked the vision to recognize what she unearthed. No one else had ever known. She'd never told Chuck. It had cost her a little money and two bad weeks last January.

"No kids," she said. "I was married only 14 months, Mag. I'm not some damned cow."

"You don't have to snap at me. I was just asking. To help."

"I don't need this cross-examination. Look, just what do you want to know?"

Maggie seemed to think. Lizabeth guessed that was what it was; her sister's brow crinkled with the effort. Maggie said, "What will you do now?" and Lizabeth knew her sister had balked before whatever mystery she'd actually wanted to explore.

"I don't know. I don't know what I'll do now. What will *you* do now?"

Maggie brightened and smiled. She was a pretty girl, Lizabeth noticed as if for the first time, the kind in ads selling shampoo or douche. Butterflies might land on her shoulders. "This is going to be a great semester."

"It is."

"Uh-huh. I'm almost done with my requirements, and the sorority is going to have a great year. I just know it."

Lizabeth stared blankly at her sister until the younger woman's smile faded. "The sorority."

Maggie hesitated. "At least I hope it will be a good semester."

"We can always hope." She'd waited long enough. Lizabeth reached into her shirt pocket and found the crushed pack of cigarettes and the crumpled pack of matches. She took tiny pleasure seeing Maggie's nose crease.

"And I have a boyfriend."

"You do."

"I think I do. Robert. Robert wrote me a bunch of letters this summer, and he was here in July. Just before . . . before you came back. You should have met him. He's real cool."

Lizabeth leaned forward off the swing, her elbows braced on her knees. Maggie was waiting to be picked up to play tennis. She wore lipstick, blush and shadow, all very subdued. The pink laces of her Reeboks matched the pom-poms of her socks.

"Cool."

"Yes."

Cool. What was cool about *cool?* "You like him?"

"Of course I do."

"What do you mean, 'Of course'?"

"I just do."

"Why?"

"He's nice."

Robert was nice and Robert was cool. Who could want more?

Maggie added, "You know, he holds doors open. Stuff like that. He wants to be a poet, but he's studying law."

"You've slept with him?"

"Liz!"

"Sister to sister. Come on, you can tell me."

Maggie looked out the screen door. Her friends were late. Her thumbnail went to her lips, but when she realized what she was doing she sharply pulled her hand away. "Sort of," she said.

"'Sort of'? What does that mean?"

"Well, everything but. You know."

Lizabeth knew exactly. She was about to say that she had no idea for the simple pleasure of hearing her sister stutter through an explanation, snagged by the obligation to explain because she'd first invoked sisterly intimacy, but a horn honked in the street before the house. Maggie grabbed her tennis racket. Lizabeth followed her sister out to the driveway.

As though they required any brief opportunity to escape a car's murky interior to stand in the sun, three girls leaned against the open doors of a pale green station wagon. Like Maggie, each was dressed in whites. Scarves tied back their hair. Lizabeth would have sworn that despite the distance the sea air carried the aromas of perfume and makeup thicker than honey on hot bread. Maggie reached the car and waved good-bye. Her black hair flew about her face. Four doors thudded shut. Without thinking about it, Lizabeth returned the wave. Maggie smiled. Automatically, Lizabeth noticed Maggie was the prettiest. Easily the prettiest.

Good for her. Good for Maggie. It was what her sister needed; it was what she had.

The wagon bounced at the driveway's end and was away. Lizabeth lowered her hand. She let herself think how if she had had anything left, anything at all, she'd have given it to be in that car, but then she thought of what she did have, how it made her stronger, and no, no, no, she would hold that to her forever.

Visit

Mostly when Harley thinks about the old days, Harley thinks about the girls he might have known. He is driving the Ford station wagon he and his good wife, Marilyn, purchased three years ago. Last month, separating the final payment coupon from the booklet, Harley experienced triumph. The muffler is nearly shot, and the brakes fade too quickly. The alternator has been replaced twice, and each time it went it took the battery with it. The damndest thing: the car was fine until 700 miles past the warranty expiration. They'd wanted a white station wagon, but since they were buying at the end of the production year, when prices are cheapest, they had to take what the dealer had on the lot, the best of which was maroon. When the sun is strong, as it is today, the vinyl seats cling and are uncomfortable. Harley has said again and again he will never buy another car without cloth seats. He is firm about this.

Harley, Marilyn, and their two boys—Rick and Art, nine and four— are on their way to Marilyn's Aunt Bea's. They take this journey once a month or so, for no special purpose. Marilyn was raised by Bea at Marilyn's father's request after Marilyn's mother passed on when Marilyn was only five years old. In the rear of the car is Ranger, their mostly-Irish-Setter-and-very-good-with-the-children dog. At the time they bought the Ford, they had thought they would need a wagon: Marilyn was pregnant, but she lost the baby. Harley is thirty-two and Marilyn is thirty. They discussed it, and they decided that Marilyn will avoid another pregnancy. Two boys it is, and two boys it will be. Sometimes Marilyn thinks how nice it would have been to brush the hair of a little girl, but she does not think about that too often, having so little time. They are all together for breakfast, Harley insists on that, and after she and Art walk Rick to the school bus stop each weekday morning, there is the housework—her three men produce a ton of laundry— the marketing, meeting Rick again at the bus stop at three-thirty, then carting him to the scout meeting or soccer practice or whatever, then back home to start dinner, out again to retrieve Rick once more, home in time to have dinner on the table for Harley when he gets in at seven, and then joining Harley in the living room for an hour or two of television once the boys have been put to bed. And there are the interrupting telephone calls from the other mothers in the development. It is a wonder she gets anything done at all. Throughout the day she conscientiously tries hard to give attention to Art. Hers is a full life, and she is content. Often she blesses herself that they had the good luck to have bought a house all on a single level. Stairs would have been her death. And they were so young when they bought the place—Rick was a babe in arms!—that they never would have thought that stairs could be a consideration. The only problems with the house are that the thin plasterboard walls make Harley and Marilyn cautious and tentative in their lovemaking now that Rick is getting so big—little pitchers have big ears!—and the walls at the rear of the house that front the sloping hill in the backyard seep dampness.

It is October. The trees are close on the twisting county road that climbs the gentle hills to Aunt Bea's, and the leaves are turning. Marilyn points out the startling flashes of russet and gold to Art, but older Rick is less impressed, happily occupied with slapping and reslapping Ranger's nose. Ranger barks loudly. Harley hears little of this, being preoccupied with the delicate navigation of the station wagon which does not handle curves well, thoughts of the girls he might have known, and wondering just when he will have to lower the boom on Doris, the salesgirl at one of the better jewelry shops in the shopping mall of which he is the manager. Once or twice a week he finds himself in a motel room with Doris during her lunch break. The affair has been going on for three months, and that is long enough. Harley considers himself a decent man, and so he must be fair to Doris and call a halt before things become a mess. He does not want her too attached to him. They have an understanding. He had the identical understanding with Marva, who sold greeting cards, and with Lucille, the hair stylist, and so he expects no difficulty with Doris.

The mall is an outstanding place to work, and he does an outstanding job. Traffic last year was up for the third year in a row, their vacancy rate is low, and the management of the anchor department stores at each end of the mall is pleased with Harley. There is talk of moving him to a larger place now under construction, though he has not mentioned this to Marilyn as the new mall will be in another state. There is no point to upsetting her until there is reason to do so. Two weeks ago the mall management boldly embarked on a plan to increase the parking area by constructing a three-storey parking area. Harley feels good when some radical decision needs to be made and he is strong enough to make it. Other people were involved, of course, but his opinion carried the most weight. They are building the first high-rise parking lot within a hundred miles.

During the forty-five minutes to Aunt Bea's the boys always get antsy, so Harley drives a tad too quickly for Marilyn's taste for the final five miles, but they arrive safely. Bea's Mercedes is parked in the driveway, but behind it is another car, a sporty little foreign job that Harley does not recognize, fire-engine red, the top down. Ranger runs across the lawn with Rick and Art in pursuit, raising flurries of leaves. As Harley passes the strange car, his fingertips drift to the top of the driver's seat. Genuine leather. Black, smooth and supple as skin. The air smells of autumn.

Bea greets them at the door, having heard the Ford pull into the driveway, and she stoops to gather Rick and Art to her ample chest while Ranger jumps and barks. Harley has his hand shaken and Marilyn is lightly embraced as the boys tear through the house straight for the kitchen where they know fresh-baked toll house cookies await them. Every time they visit Bea, the boys have no appetite by dinner time, and though Harley again and again has asked Marilyn to admonish Bea, Marilyn remains silent. Harley endures this.

The grown-ups head for Bea's den, a precisely decorated room with a working fireplace Harley has never seen lighted. Harley always looks at the floor-to-ceiling oak bookshelf for the photograph of Bea's long-dead husband, who Marilyn barely remembers, a fellow named Rob. In the photograph he wears a fedora at a jaunty angle, has a foot propped on the bumper of a 1948 Buick, and is smiling into the camera for all the world, thinks Harley, as though he expects to live forever. Bea has not led a quiet life, and Harley wonders just how many men the old boy in the photograph has had to gaze upon as they sipped a drink or two in this den. Marilyn, when she has had a few, will with a note of wonder in her voice sometimes tell Harley the story of this one or that one and how he treated Bea. Though Bea had a thousand boy-friends, Marilyn remembers each of them by name, at least the ones she got to meet. Bea's money is a mystery to Harley. The house, the grounds, her way of life: the best he can figure is that her husband died overinsured. So he enters the den, looks to the photo, and glows with warmth at the thought of the whole-life policy he carries for a quarter-mil.

Seated on the soft velour-covered love seat are what must be the owners of the red sports car. Harley first notices the woman is beautiful and blonde, and then his attention swings to the man close beside her. He is athletic and tanned, his white tennis shirt flat upon his chest and abdomen, his beige slacks neatly creased down to his soft leather loaf-ers. A touch of gray spots his hair, and crow's feet are at the corners of his blue eyes. He drinks what appears to be scotch. He does not stand when Harley, Marilyn, and Bea enter the den, but extends his hand, slightly moist from holding the glass, to Harley, who gives it his best two-shake firm grasp and gets about the same in return. Bea makes introductions.

Elliot and Laura are recently moved into the three-floor Tudor house further up the road. Harley notices there is no wedding ring on his or her hand, and the gentility of Bea's omission of a last name is not lost on him. Elliot must be fifty-ish, and Laura may be twenty-five. Her eyes are also blue.

Bea waves at Harley to help himself to a drink. At the wet bar in the corner of the den, Ranger nuzzles him from behind and a bit of scotch sloshes over the glass's edge wetting his wrist. While he pours Mari-lyn's sweet vermouth on the rocks, the dog leaps onto the love seat, upsetting Elliot and long-haired Laura. He hears Laura laugh, and Marilyn scolds the dog. Ranger's paws scuttle across the waxed parquet floor and the dog whirls away to find the boys. Harley turns with the two drinks in his hand, taking pleasure from the cold smooth feel of

Bea's generous-sized old-fashioned glasses, and he crosses the room to sit on a director's chair between Marilyn and Bea at the chrome and glass bridge table.

Elliot and Laura are just returned from two weeks in Nassau where Elliot "actually did a round in seventy-eight" and "dropped a few dollars" at the crap tables. Marilyn mentions that their last vacation was in a tent with the boys up at the lake, and Harley quickly adds they are planning to get away just by themselves as soon as his job permits it. He is grateful when Marilyn does not mention this is news to her, but only looks at him with one eyebrow slightly cocked. Laura, he decides, is definitely no more than twenty-five, and may be the best-looking woman he has ever seen outside of a magazine. She makes Doris the salesgirl look like a refugee from a kennel, and there is simply no point in comparing her to Marilyn. Laura wears a bright pink skirt, and her legs are crossed at the knees. Harley imagines her long hair flying out behind her as the sports car speeds along a twisting forested road. She'd wear a T-shirt, he imagines, and shorts, and that long slender right leg would hang lazily over the passenger door, her foot bare.

Marilyn tells about their sons, age, grade, energy levels, and so forth, and Elliot smiles, Laura smiles, and Harley finds himself smiling, too. No, Elliot and Laura have no children, they say. They've plenty of time for that, says Bea. Laura blushes prettily.

When Marilyn suddenly becomes perturbed because she has not heard a sound from the boys for a few minutes, she and Bea leave the room. Harley smiles. Elliot smiles. Laura swirls her drink, the ice tinkling.

I'm in management, Harley says. Commercial properties. The shopping mall.

Elliot says, Investments.

A broker?

No, an investor. He smiles. His teeth are perfect.

Laura leans against Elliot's shoulder. Harley notices her breast flatten against Elliot's lean arm. Harley's glass is empty. He walks across the room and pours himself a strong one, less water, and offers Bea's guests a refill.

Laura defers to Elliot, and Elliot says, No. They have to be leaving in a few minutes, anyway, a tennis appointment.

I used to play tennis, Harley says.

Did you? says Elliot.

Elliot and Laura make their excuses. The two men shake hands again, and this time Harley squeezes harder, but so does Elliot, and so the grip is a standoff. Laura offers Harley a limp hand, and he takes it, softer than any of his imagined memories. He hears Marilyn shout a farewell—she is preoccupied with the boys—and then the front door shuts. The engine of the sports car is a throaty growl. He hears it shift gears twice, then the sound fades into the wooded suburb.

The day at Bea's goes as it always does. Bea offers to cook, but Harley and Marilyn implore her not to. Harley takes Rick and drives the station wagon into town, and they buy rye bread, sliced turkey, and potato salad. Harley prepares his sandwich with a great deal of mayonnaise. Art drops food to Ranger, though Marilyn admonishes him not to do so. Bea laughs. Bea mentions that she is planning another cruise, this time around the Greek islands, but she has doubts about such an arduous trip. Marilyn encourages her. Harley eats slowly, deliberately, smiling at appropriate moments, trying to imagine what Laura and Elliot look like in bed together. They'd look good. He watches Marilyn, and thinks how that night he will want her.

The boys sleep in the car when they drive home. The garage door opens when Marilyn presses the electronic signal, and closes automatically after three minutes. Marilyn carries Art, Harley carries Rick. Ranger trots tiredly into the living room. Art doesn't awaken as Marilyn puts him into pajamas, though Rick sleepily opens his eyes, insists on brushing his teeth as he was taught to do in school, and then the boys are tucked beneath their blankets. Rick rolls to his side before Harley has a chance to kiss him, and so he kisses only the back of his older son's head.

Harley and Marilyn stand at the door of their sons' room. Harley's arm circles his wife's waist. They close the door of the children's room. Marilyn asks if he is hungry, and Harley says he is not. He'd like to get to bed.

But Marilyn could go for a snack. She heads for the kitchen. He goes to the master bathroom, showers, brushes his teeth, and combs his hair.

Just as he is about to step into the bedroom, he returns to the bathroom vanity and slaps aftershave onto his cheeks and chest.

In his robe, he lies on top of the sheet and waits for Marilyn. He handles the cool chrome of the television's remote control, but does not turn the set on. The lamp beside the bed glows dimly. Marilyn comes in carrying the remains of half a cheese sandwich. She places it on the night table.

While she showers, Harley again thinks of Laura, and bitterly thinks of Elliot. Where do guys like that get it? Why are they entitled? He works hard, is a good provider. Ranger scratches at the bedroom door. The dog whines. After a short time that stops, as Harley knew it would. He thinks of surprising Marilyn in the shower, but makes no move to get up, sure that the moment he opens the stall door she will chase him away. Marilyn is a terrific companion, a great mother, and has no adventure in her soul, a fact Harley believes in some respects may be a virtue. Her orgasms are small, intense, private little affairs, predictable and unmysterious. He wonders if Laura is a screamer. He'd bet she's a screamer. She has perfect teeth, too.

Marilyn is stark naked when she enters the bedroom. Her full breasts, still damp from the shower, glisten. Her waist is not as narrow as it once was. Her dark hair is tied up in a towel. She sits on the bed's edge and eats the last of her cheese sandwich, then undoes the towel wrapping her hair. When she bends forward to brush it out, Harley can count the vertebrae of her spine down to the spread of her bottom. Though Laura was darkly tanned, Harley is sure her skin is naturally pale, pink, and transluscent.

Marilyn replaces her hairbrush onto the night table, sits still a moment, and then switches off the lamp. Harley feels her move in the darkness, lying down beside him. He rolls to his hip, shedding his robe. His arm goes across her chest. She moves away from him, lifting his arm.

I was thinking, she says. I was thinking about that couple we met.

What about them? Harley says.

He's much older than she is. I thought so. He is much older, isn't he?

I guess so, Harley says. I hadn't thought about it.

He reaches for her again, and she rolls away from him.

I was just thinking, Marilyn says.

Harley nuzzles her neck.

No, Harley, Marilyn says. Cut it out. I'm all wound up with Bea and the boys and all. I'm just too tense. And I was thinking about that couple. I was thinking, I'll bet they're horribly unhappy. They didn't look like happy people, did they? I don't think they're happy. I'd bet that's why Bea is trying to make friends. She takes people in like that.

I'm sure you're right, Harley says. They looked absolutely miserable to me, too.

His hand kneads the soft flesh of her neck. After a while of this, she relents and turns toward Harley. Quietly, she whispers, the boys. Quietly. God, I am so lucky. We are so very lucky.

Away Out and Over

Before Kyle vanished one rainy Tuesday, he'd affected Hadley in only two perceptible ways. In college Hadley had smoked an occasional mentholated cigarette. Now, like Kyle, she smoked unfiltered Camels and, as she spoke, she unselfconsciously peeled small shreds of tobacco from her teeth and tongue. The other effect of seven years with Kyle was Simon, four years old with the enormous dark eyes and unruly straight black hair of his father. A quiet child, Simon clung always to his mother's hand or knee. Hadley was not at all given to flamboyance or an exaggerated sense of the dramatic, so she was all the more astonished when she conceived the idea of sealing herself and Simon in an oil drum, setting themselves adrift, and washing in a graceful arc over the edge of Niagara Falls.

There had been no question of foul play in Kyle's disappearance. The day before, their two bank accounts had been emptied. He'd left the van in the driveway and some of his suits in the closet. There had been no note. He'd given no notice at the office, nor did they know of any reason he should have left. For a while Hadley had believed there was some explanation. Spies, or blackmail perhaps. She'd already forgiven him, however obscene the act he'd committed. When she articulated her beliefs, her friends smiled, nodded, and then exchanged concerned glances among themselves. During that initial period, her friends visited often—always in groups of three or more. They agreed that Hadley was remarkably composed. After a month with no word, Hadley finally acknowledged financial reality. She began searching for a job. She had a degree in Art History and knew quite a bit about Seurat.

After two weeks of looking for work, her legs grew achy from unaccustomed heels, none of the employment agencies with which she'd
filed had yet called her, and her initial optimism was displaced by her
gradual concession, reinforced by at least a dozen personnel officers,
that her lack of experience or marketable skills were not compensated
for by her enthusiasm or the speed at which she said she learned. She
took a day to rest, a second, and then a third. During that interval the
idea of sweeping over the Falls welled spontaneously within her. It was
the only possibility, and something had to be done.

One morning, she put Simon into jeans and a rugby shirt, attempted
to brush the hair from his eyes, loaded him into the van, and drove the
two blocks to Phyllis's. Hadley reasoned that Phyllis should have several good suggestions because Phyllis's husband was an architect and
that was almost an engineer.

Phyllis's two girls were at school. She went about in a blue flannel
robe, which was missing two buttons. When Phyllis padded across the
kitchen to pour the remainder of the morning's coffee into the sink, the
mules on her feet slapped at her heels. Through the window came the
rhythmic creak of a rusty swing in the backyard where Simon enter-
tained himself. Phyllis's eyes were cinder gray. While she talked she
habitually puffed breath up across her face, jouncing the frosted bangs
over her forehead.

"Coffee? Or something with a kick?"

"Why not?"

"Good. Me too."

Phyllis took one tumbler from the sink and another from the cabinet.
The glasses clinked full with ice; a lime was sliced into eight segments.
She withdrew a near-full pitcher from the refrigerator, poured two
Bloody Marys, set the pitcher beside the ashtray, and sat opposite Had-
ley. They smoked and drank until Phyllis leaned forward and said,

"I want to ask you something."

"Go ahead."

"I don't want you to think I'm—you know—pushy or anything."

"Go ahead, Phyll. It's okay."

Phyllis took a deep breath. "Have you called a lawyer or something?
You know—to see what you can do."

"About what?"

"You know. Kyle."

"For what?" Her tongue felt nicely fuzzy.

"God, Hadley, I don't know how you stand it. I swear I don't. If Ted did that to me I'd find him and—I don't know what. But I swear he'd bleed. Jesus. I always thought you were more ballsy."

Hadley finished her drink. "Kyle must have had his reasons. I'm not bitter or anything. I'm really not." Her glass refilled. "I don't feel anything."

"Uh-huh."

"I don't."

"If you say so," Phyllis sighed. They traded miscellaneous gossip and talk, smoked and drank for a time more. "That wasn't really what I wanted to ask, you know."

"I didn't think so."

"You want another?"

Was it three now? "Sure." The red stuff poured thickly over the ice.

"Had? What have you been doing for, uh, you know. What?"

The kitchen had grown warm and Hadley was feeling stupid with the heat. She didn't understand. "For what?"

"Jesus. You know." Phyllis leaned over the table, her drink circled by her arms. Her robe fell open. "For jollies. I mean, you know, what are you doing to get your cookies off?"

Oh. That. Hadley giggled. "You mean sex."

They giggled together.

"Why, for heaven's sake, don't you just say 'sex'?"

Phyllis started to explain but giggled helplessly. It infected Hadley. Each time they tried to talk they liquified into laughter. Sex was very funny. No, Hadley had not thought about it.

"Really. Really. Stop now. I really want to know, Had. Really! God! I mean you get out. I sat for Simon a few times. Have you found someone? A few someones? Go to one of those single places yet? God, I'd like to get over to the city. My sister tells me about this place. Sounds fabulous. And so—so!"

"Phyll?"

"Yes?"

"I don't do anything."

"What?" Phyllis said sleepily.

"I said 'I don't do anything.' For sex, I mean."

"Nothing?"

"No. Nothing."

"Well, why not? I mean, Jesus, why not?" Phyllis reached for the pitcher. It was empty. "Damn." She started to rinse it, but it fell from her shaking hand and shattered in the sink. "Damn. Waterford. You should, Had. You should." She picked at the shards of glass.

"Should what?"

"You depress me. It's not right. It's not natural. Nothing? Really?"

"Nothing."

"I'd die by myself. Go nuts."

"I'm sure I can make it alone. It's a matter of finding what I can do."

Phyllis flapped her hand. "Damn it, now I've cut myself. Help with this glass and watch your fingers."

The screen door banged closed. Simon, awaiting permission to speak, watched them darkly from the door.

"Yes, dear?"

"I have to make."

"It's upstairs, honey," Phyllis said. The boy went up the stairs. "What about Simon?"

"What about Simon? I don't know about Simon. He'll make out. Kids always do. I don't know about Simon." He was back, silent, framed in the doorway. "Did you wash?"

"Yes."

"Go outside. Play some more."

"I'm tired. There's no one to play with."

"Just a while, pussy."

He left. The screen door slammed closed again. They heard the rusty squeak of the swing. Hadley ignited a Camel.

"Listen. I came over to talk to you about an idea I have."

"You want something to eat? Cheese? Peanuts?"

"No. Listen, Phylly, please."

Phyllis drifted through the kitchen, lifting an object here, setting it there, straightening jars which were not askew, wiping already clean counters.

"I've thought of what I'm going to do, maybe."

"Oh?"

"Yes. It's probably a little crazy, but I think I can. Phyll? Are you listening? I think I'm going to go over Niagara Falls. Isn't that crazy?"

"Well, why not? It's nice this time of year. All the leaves. Colors. I went to Niagara Falls once. God! It was so long ago. I was still in school and this boy, a beautiful boy. . . ."

"No. No. You don't understand. Not *to* the Falls, *over* the Falls. In a barrel. Or a can. An oil can."

"You mean a drum."

"Right. An oil drum. What do you think? Me and Simon go over Niagara Falls. God. That drop. I can feel my stomach go. Out and over. It should get a lot of publicity and maybe we'll even be on the talk shows and I can tell everybody my side of it. I can get some money that way, and there will be a book I guess. Royalties. Phil Donahue. You worked for a publisher, right? People want to read about that kind of thing, don't they?"

Phyllis's eyes shown like vanilla glaze on a cupcake. "Movie rights. In the office, all they ever talked about was movie rights." She sucked her injured thumb.

"Movie rights? I hadn't thought. It's not like people do it all the time. I figured next week. Maybe Kyle will read about it in the papers. Next week. Do you think I can play myself in the movie? No. I couldn't. Candice Bergen. Yes. She'd be perfect. I'm not right for myself. Simon can be Simon. I don't see why not. He doesn't talk much, anyway." She crushed her cigarette into the ashtray.

Phyllis propped herself against the refrigerator. "Have you tested it out yet?"

"What?"

"A drum. Barrel. Whatever. Have you tested one? How much air is in an empty oil drum?"

"Should be enough."

"Sure. But test it first. That's what Ted would do. My Ted, the builder." She slid again into a giggle fit.

It was just the thing. Test it first. It was too hard to think of everything alone.

"I could put Simon in the barrel to see how long the air lasts. First five minutes. Then ten. Then fifteen. Like that. Simon won't mind. Nothing bothers that kid."

"Right. That's the stuff. Scientifical."

"Right. Right. Where the hell is Simon?" Hadley stood unsteadily and peered through the horizontal frosted slats of the window. The October sun was bright and hurt her eyes. Simon sat on the immobile swing. He talked to the air. "I'm going to get the kid."

Phyllis waved. "G'head. Go on. Go on. I'm all right. Take care. Call. Hey, Had?"

"Yes?"

"Go to a bar. Please."

The screen door banged. Simon was small and alone in the backyard. Like his father, he was able to sit without company for long periods. Hadley seized control of herself—the fresh air helped—and she made her way across the ragged lawn. Simon's large dark eyes held her as she came.

"Who are you talking to?"

"Daddy."

She looked around. "There's no one here. Are you sure it was Daddy?"

Simon considered the question. "I know my own Daddy."

Her fingernails drummed her hip. "Make-believe-Daddy, or Daddy-Daddy?"

His toes pushed into the dirt and the swing creaked in a lazy arc. "I thought he was real. Was he, Mommy?"

"I don't know. I don't know." Her cool fingers curled around his ear. "Come on. We've got things to do," she said impatiently. He took her hand.

The next morning was encased by a solid slate sky. Hadley did some pointless things to the house while Simon spooned cereal. He took single bites from each of two buttered slices of rye toast and then announced that he was going out to play.

"Be home for lunch."

Hadley sat on the bed and coughed her way through the third cigarette of the morning. Then, a decision made, she dressed, thought fleetingly of the dishes on the sink counter and the crumbs littering the tabletop, and climbed behind the wheel of the van. She left the door of the house unlocked in case Simon came home before she did. It was time the kid learned to take care of himself, anyway.

The van cruised. Eventually she saw what she wanted and wheeled into a service station where oil drums were pyramided against a white stucco garage wall. Bells chimed as the van's tires crushed the signal cord. She jumped from the seat.

The attendant came from the office wiping his hands on his trousers. "Fill it?"

"No thanks. I don't want gas. I need a drum."

"A what?"

"A drum. A drum. An oil drum. One of those." She pointed to the pyramid.

"They go back to the company, lady. They use them again. They ship hydraulic fluid and diesel fuel in the things."

"Oh, well, do you ever damage one? You know, lose it or something?"

"Yeah. Sure. We lose 'em sometimes."

"Okay then. Give me one. I'll pay."

"Lady, what do you want with one of them things?"

"I'm an artist. I need it for a sculpture I'm doing. It will be part of a work of art."

"What are you? Kidding?"

"Sculpture. Honest. A modern sculpture."

"I don't know."

"Five dollars?"

"It's kind of crazy and. . . ."

"Ten?"

"Well, so long as you got a van and get out of here quick. I don't want the boss should see."

"Sure."

"An artist?"

"Right. I'll need a top. The lid."

"These here?"

"That's right. They fit right on?"

"Tight, too. Just clip and twist to seal it shut. The rubber ring seals it. Nothin' can spill out. Like the clips on your suitcase, you know what I mean? To open it, you just flip them up again."

Ten minutes later she was back on the highway. She bellowed happily along with the radio. Independence was a wonderful opportunity.

The barrel was about three feet high and two across. Not enough for her and Simon, so she'd send Simon over. That was good, too. Maybe better. She could set Simon adrift at night because that way no one would see and stop her and then she'd get to the bottom of the Falls and tell people so they'd help her. When they fished him out, she'd be there. Fifteen minutes. Figure half an hour to be safe. It was good enough. They'd be all right if there was enough air for him. He might get banged around, of course, but life was like that. People get injured. The kid would have to take his chances along with everybody else.

Home, she rolled the thing into the backyard and, determined that everything be perfect, she took a box of soap pads from the kitchen. With the barrel on its side, she crawled into it. The gunk was hard to remove, but the force from her garden hose helped. In an hour, Hadley was a mess, but the drum's interior shone like an aluminum pot. She'd always been a good housekeeper. Before Kyle had left, everything in the house had been just so. She ached from the awkward postures she'd assumed and her muscles pleaded for a hot bath.

She peeled off her wet clothing and ran hot water over the pink crystals she'd sprinkled into the tub. She knelt, her hand immersed to the wrist, slowly stirring circles. She'd always been soothed by long baths, the drain open, her head filled with the roar from the faucet, her body half afloat, the water forever renewed and warm. She waited while the tub bubbled. Lately, she had not bothered with the details of looking beautiful. That would have to change if she was to be a celebrity.

She swallowed a red pill she took from the medicine chest and lowered herself into the tub. Her eyelids fell and her muscles laxed. Her hands pressed into her skin; hips, abdomen, thighs, and breasts. The porcelain was cool and wet on the back of her neck. There was no fantasy, only warm sensation. Everyone knew she had a good body, although she worried about her calves: even after Simon's birth her stomach had stayed tight and flat. She'd worked at it, too. Those situps. Everyone knew. Kyle had liked her body. Her fingernails traced spiderwebs over her stomach. She undulated to her rhythms, tensed, shuddered, and then drifted.

She soaked for an hour. Afterward, she dried herself with an enormous magenta towel, dressed, and still slightly feeling the waft of the pill, but more sure of herself than she'd been in weeks, she went to Simon's room. The kid sat cross-legged on the bone-white carpet in a circle of flickering blue television light. His back was to Hadley, and she realized he wore the same rugby shirt and jeans he'd worn the day before. That was not right, nor was it proper that his hair was all disheveled. Kyle had never combed his hair, either. She shut the television. He remained immobile on the floor, his dark eyes staring blankly at the now darkened screen. Then, as though another switch had been thrown, Simon became animated and turned his head to his mother.

"Can I have lunch now?"

"No. Not yet. We're going to try something first. A new game."

"I want cream cheese and jelly."

"Later. Get me the stopwatch Daddy gave you."

He searched the clutter of his closet. Hadley went to the backyard and stood the oil drum on end. She held the lid in her hand. Simon called from the house.

"In the back Simon."

He walked to his mother. The lace of his right sneaker was undone.

"How does this work, darling?"

"Well, you press this button here and it starts and again and it stops and again and it goes back to twelve. It's easy. What's the game? Do I have to run? I can run fast, Mommy. Daddy taught me to run fast."

"Game?"

"You said we'd play a game. You said."

"That's right, I did, didn't I? Well, Mommy wants to try something. See this? You get in and Mommy will put the top on and then I'll let you out. See?"

He examined her.

"It's very simple. Just listen to me."

"It'll be dark." He looked at his feet. His hands clasped behind him.

"You're not afraid of the dark are you?"

"No. I'm not." Simon began to cry. "Yes I am. I am. Mommy, do I have to? Do I have to get in there? Do I? I don't want to get in there. I'm scared."

She held him close. "Yes. You have to get in there. It will be all right. It's just for a little while. Do as Mommy says. Be a good boy. Be Mommy's brave little man."

Simon whimpered as Hadley lifted him by the armpits and slowly lowered him into the barrel. "Squat, dear." She fit the lid into place and snapped the stays. She pressed the silver knob of the watch. Far off, she heard him crying, but that stopped after the first sixty-seven seconds.

Hadley sat on the unmowed grass. The watch ticked. It was chilly in the backyard. She wished she'd thought to bring a sweater. Simon should have a jacket, too. Only five minutes, she thought, only five minutes the first time. The family of starlings that had been in the birdhouse were gone, she realized. Sometime during the last month they'd departed. Perhaps they'd have stayed if she thought to leave bread. Gone. Just like that. Three minutes and a few seconds had elapsed. It was wrong to use Simon like this. She sobbed at her inability to stop herself. It was a shame. Kyle should have said something to her. Anything. Even if he'd picked a stupid fight, there would have been some sense to it because she'd at least have had something to hate. The yard was quiet. She sat on the cold ground and put her ear to the barrel. There was no sound. They would paint the barrel red, white, and blue. That was showmanship and patriotism. Kyle had said there was a difference between logical and rational, and she'd never before felt the difference in herself until she heard a faint sound from within the drum, but because she couldn't be sure, she did nothing, which was absolutely logical. Six minutes and twenty-eight seconds. That was beyond what she had wanted, she'd lost track again, so what the hell? she'd try for fifteen minutes. It would be dark and cold in the barrel. Hadley wished Kyle was with her. Kyle had made good decisions for her. He had never doubted himself. She cried, her face all mucous and tears. Why couldn't she make good decisions? She was all alone, like Simon all alone. Nine minutes and thirty-seven seconds. It's not fair to be all alone. There should be something more besides the dark cold of the barrel and the roar of Niagara Falls. She rocked, her knees clasped to her chest.

She became aware of her hunger. Hadley placed the still-running stopwatch atop the barrel and went into the kitchen. She made herself a grilled cheese sandwich and, because she'd been drinking too much coffee recently, and that made her hands shake, she poured herself a glass of milk. She turned on the radio and sat at the table by the window where she ate and waited to hear a report. The window overlooked the backyard.

The news came on. Hadley was, at first, puzzled there was no report. Then she felt silly. Of course, no one knew, so there could be no report. She would have to make a phone call and then it would be on the news and Kyle would hear and he'd know that he should never have left. He'd return then, understand, they'd cry a little, and everything would be fine. She could forgive him.

She placed the last bit of her sandwich in her mouth, wiped her fingers with a yellow napkin, and looked out the window to the yard where the barrel stood in the stark late afternoon sun. The morning's clouds had dispersed. She went to the telephone. Certainly, the Falls would have been more spectacular, but Hadley was completely pleased with herself. If a woman can just stay in control and bring her intelligence to bear on a problem, then there is no difficulty so great she must feel inadequate.

Easily and Well

Dear Mr. Burnam,

How are you? I am fine, I think. You said I should write, so here goes. I've been here for three weeks and it's even better than I ever imagined. The college is really beautiful. I feel as though I am in Central Park all the time. It's perfect. The older buildings look like tiny cool dark castles, and when I walk into them I feel hushed, as though I've entered a bank or something. The dorms are modern, mostly glass and concrete, but comfy. As usual, you were right when you said I should go to a small school. Everybody seems friendly. After three years with just grandma, I finally have a family again.

I'm taking regular freshman classes: English (the professor isn't half as interesting as you), Classical Civ., Spanish (which is easy for me), Intro. to Psych., and a class in Dance. Most of my classes are OK, but I love Dance. I'm sure I'll be able to keep my scholarship.

My roommate is all right. Ann from Westchester smokes grass all day long, has lots of clothes, but wears jeans and a black sweatshirt. We're very different and so have lots to talk about. Ann said she doesn't mind living with a clean Puerto Rican and I said Jews are mostly OK and we both laughed. Like a family. She was really knocked out to hear I'd gone to an all-girls school—she said I must be flaky because of it, but I told her I've always been weird. Actually, having boys in class doesn't bother me much. They're mostly regular people.

Just before, I was looking through my yearbook, remembering. Everybody signed this ridiculous stuff about always keeping in touch, but

I won't hear from any of them and I don't really care. All the teachers wrote "Best Wishes" or something else they could scribble quickly. Except you. Yours is really beautiful. I still feel warm when I read it. Even though you were a teacher, you were my best friend in high school. All those long talks in your office. I've made a needlepoint of one part of what you wrote and it is hanging over my bed. "Love Easily And Well If Not Wisely." I added the capitals.

Give my love to your wife and child. The two times I had dinner at your home were very important to me. I don't get much mail. My grandma doesn't know how to write and my folks are far away in PR and probably don't care anyway. Things have never been good for them. If it isn't too much bother, please send me a letter. But if you don't, I'll understand.

Peace,
Rita Montanez

Oct. 20

Dear Mr. B.,

I was very depressed when your letter arrived and that cheered me up. Nothing specific, just my usual blahs. You've talked me out of my blahs many times, and hearing from you makes me feel like you're here and we're talking again. I always feel different from everyone else. I dress the way I do because I like to, and I speak directly because I don't know any other way to speak. You once said to me that all my differences were positive, that eventually I'd meet someone who appreciated my craziness, and that I should cling to my individuality. Still, it's hard being so alone.

My roommate is getting on my nerves. Ann is always stoned and is impossible to talk with. Two weeks ago she didn't sleep in our room for three nights. Her parents kept calling and I had to make excuses why she wasn't in. When she came back, I told her how embarrassed I was, but all she did was shrug like it was my problem. So we finally had a serious talk and she asked me if I was gay. When she left, I cried. I'm thinking of asking for a single room. If I get it, I'll send you my new address.

In my Psych course we are reading about defense mechanisms and compulsive behavior. It all sounds so right, I hate it. Everybody is in all these boxes and they know just what we are going to do next. I hate it. How can anyone be spontaneous with Old Sigmund looking over her shoulder? I'm into Aristophanes. Beowulf is only OK.

In your letter you said not to let school get in the way of my education and that if I wrote to you I should talk about what your "favorite wide-eyed innocent" was doing, but not in class. That made me smile. You are always able to see and understand so much about me, more than I can. Right off you got to the core of things. I met Bill last week. He was alone sunning himself on the grass and reading Keats and since I've read the Odes (in your class) I went over and introduced myself. I've always imagined it would be like that. Poetry, and a boy lying on the grass. Bill has these soulful brown eyes, not deep like yours, but kind of innocent and vulnerable. We had beers that night and danced a little and I thought he really liked me, so when he asked, I went with him to his room. The next day he was different. I was really surprised and a little hurt. It doesn't seem right for someone who reads Keats.

I guess he's the reason I've been in a funk. I don't really care about him, I decided. He's no great loss. And—it's strange, I don't feel funny writing this to you—my virginity was no big deal. You once said not to rush things and I haven't. It happened when it did and I didn't feel forced by circumstances. He needed me, and even if that was only for one night, that's fine.

Writing to you helps me think things out.

I've cut my hair short and am wearing it in a 'fro like Mrs. Burnam's. It feels funny after having had hair all the way down my back, but tell her she is right; it's much easier to take care of.

I have some reading to do now, so I guess that's all for this letter. Take care.

Rita

Dec. 15

Mr. B.,

I'm sorry I took so long to write to you. I hope you're not angry, but

I've been so incredibly busy I just haven't had the chance. I know you'll understand. So much has happened I don't know where to start, but first I'll respond to what you wrote.

Yes, of course I'm taking birth control pills. They give them out at the school clinic. I'm eighteen now, and if, as you say, I left high school "sexually unsophisticated," I'm not a complete dope, either. There are things besides fucking, and at an all-girls public school in New York City there were certainly enough pregnant people waddling about for me not to believe "it can't happen to me." Sometimes the phrases you use make me giggle.

As for "getting a reputation," it's just not like that. It *is* a small college, eight hundred students, and everyone *does* know everyone else's business, but I guess things are different from when you were in school. It's casual. I can see your eyebrows now, the way you raised them and scowled at me whenever you thought I said something outrageous, but trust me. No one *cares* that much anymore who sleeps with who. Communication is what matters. How can you think sex erodes friendship?

I wasn't hurt because Bill and I had "a one-night stand," and I did not "naturally feel used," but I *was* upset because I thought I had found someone I could really relate to, but learned I'd made a mistake. It feels funny writing about Bill. That was a long time ago and he was just a boy.

Some of these insights I have learned from Alex (short for Alexis, not Alexander) who was up here for a month giving a series of Sociology lectures. I suppose that is the advantage of this "exclusive" school that gave a scholarship to this minority student: we can afford to ship in the best. Alex spoke about urban schools and minority students, so when I saw the publicity posters, I went. There was this man from North Carolina with a doctorate, and everything he said was *wrong!* After the lecture I went up and told him he was crazy, and he laughed until I explained that I was one of the people he was talking about. It always surprises people, I guess because I'm pale and don't have much of an accent. Alex took me out for coffee and we talked for a long time, at first about me and my background, and then about him. Alex is thirty-two and married, but we both could instantly feel that didn't matter. We had a fine relationship for the two weeks before he had to return to North Carolina. He called me his "sociological sport." The important thing, the reason I'm telling you this, is that we related. I could tell he needed me. We were very warm, a blend of personalities, and I'll never regret any of it. He may be back next year, and if he comes, he'll be looking for me. Alex is sad, in a way. His wife can't have any children and they are both so involved in their academic careers (she teaches Statistics) that they are growing away from each other. Even if it was short, our relationship was deep—and duration is not as important as depth.

You can't believe the snow up here. The campus looks like a Christmas card, all glittering white, and the snow *stays* clean. Incredible. Bob (a good friend from Dance who is fabulously talented) and I were walking from class across the main quad and we started to run because it felt like the thing to do. The snow was so high we got exhausted and collapsed. We couldn't get up we were laughing so hard. Then some people threw snowballs at us, and in ten minutes everyone on campus was involved in this humongous snowball fight. Afterward, Bob made cocoa. I never knew hot chocolate could be so good.

If things work out, I may be coming in for Christmas week. In all the time I've been here I've had one dreary letter from my folks and have spoken to grandma only once on the phone. I feel distant from them all, but Christmas is Christmas. If I can, when I'm in the city, I'll call you.

If you write, send the letter to the address on the envelope c/o Mr. Robert Abrams. I've moved out of the dorm.

Be good.

Rita

P.S. I promise I'll try to call you "Tom" next letter I write. I'm just not ready for that. You're still "Mr. Burnam."

Love,
R.

Jan. 10-12

Dear Tom,

It's two o'clock in the morning, I've been studying for finals, and everything is in the pits.

Seeing you was wonderful and terrible all at once. I've thought a lot about what you said, I really have, it upset me a great deal, but I still think you're mostly wrong. It's important to me that you understand, so I'll try once more. You looked shocked when I told you I'd slept with seven men since school began (I don't write *everything*) but I don't think I've gone "off the deep end." Yes, on the surface it looks like what you said, but each time it felt right—and feelings are more important than appearances. I was disturbed when you said I might be guilty of self-deception in my relations with men. Maybe you are right that I should sleep with someone *I* want, as opposed to someone I think needs *me*. I'll try it. I promise. But it's difficult for me to know the difference. If, as you said, part of my craziness is that I've no clear idea of who I am and so it is easier for me to be what other people want, and that I am "a woman of responses with no assertive will," then all I can say is, "So what?" You always put things so strongly, it's hard to argue, but please believe me, I'm comfortable with what I am doing. I am. That's the part you are wrong about. I don't feel shitty about myself. I like me.

I felt awful when you said you felt some guilt for my behavior. I cannot believe you when you say, "all that humanistic crap about self-actualization and freedom" was the "response of a middle-class white teacher confronting poverty," a "strategy to open the eyes of deprived young people to their own potential," and was never meant to be taken as "a justification for total personal license." Don't deny a word. I've a high IQ and a hell of a memory. You were trying to wipe the cocktail sauce from your shirt cuff at the time. Sometimes you talk like one of Alex's books (he's written two). You sounded horribly unnatural, as though you'd rehearsed a speech.

It was odd to be with you in that bar, and I saw a side of you I'd never dreamed existed. In high school you were always so certain of everything, so lucid, and there you were groping for words and phrases, correcting yourself, stammering, with your shirt cuff in the shrimp cocktail. That's why I don't believe you. Not the shrimp (Did the stain come out? Did you tell Mrs. Burnam to use lemon juice?). I don't believe what you said because it's always easy to say what you truly believe. You taught me that. And there you were, tongue-tied. Thanks for trying; it shows you really care. I wish I could hug you. But please,

Tom, don't feel guilty. You're a strong influence on me, more than even you think, but you're not the only influence.

You also asked me to think about how I've changed since I started school and to consider if I was pleased with those changes. I have. This may surprise you, but I still think of myself as alone. Loneliness has nothing to do with having people around; it's something at my very center. You are one of the few people who have ever touched me there. You once told me I was intelligent, sensitive, but nondirected. I suppose the big change is that I am close to knowing the things I want. Don't ask me what those things are. I'm unsure myself. They're just beyond realization, unformed as smoke, but any second they'll get solid and I'll be able to grab them. The change is that when I was a kid, last year, I didn't even know they were there. And yes, I'm pleased.

I'm sure that is not the sort of change you had in mind when you gave me my "homework assignment," but that seems to me to be the only significant change.

Am I making any sense?

I'm crying as I write this because I want you to know me. For a year I saw you every day and I never felt closer to anyone. You always understood so much without me having to explain it to death. We are on the same wavelength. Seeing you made me realize how much I've missed you. I was nervous on my way to the bar, but when you smiled and said I looked as funky as ever, it was just like it always had been. At least it was for me.

I wish you'd tell me more of what happens in your head. The only time I got some idea was a time in your office, I'm sure you don't remember, you off-handedly said you hoped I would never wake up someday when I was twenty-eight (your age at the time) and then realize I'd lost the courage to take the necessary chances to do great things. You looked so sad. God, how I cried for you that night! Why haven't you done anything about that feeling? Twenty-eight isn't old. You're too good to be doing what you're doing where you are. What great things did you miss? Why not now? God, it's so late and I have an exam at 8:00.

(It's two days later and I've read this letter and I'm unsure I'll mail it.)

I did OK on my exam, I think. May Sir Gawain and the Green Knight both rot. In March, the Dance Troupe is doing a show—three performances. I'm in it and I'd love for you to drive up. I could show you around. I'd like that a lot. If it's a problem of expense, I'm sure I can get you a room.

Say Hi to Mrs. Burnam for me and tell her I'm sorry you couldn't work it out that I could see her, too, over Christmas.

Love,

Rita

Feb. 28

Dear Tom,

I've waited until now to write. Did you get my last letter? Please drop me a letter when you can. How are things at our dear old high school? It's supercold up here. I'm sick of snow. I'm living in the dorms again. I got a single this term. The address is on the envelope. I've just got time for this short note. I'm due at rehearsal.

Yours,

Rita

Mar. 9

Dear Tom,

I got your long letter this morning, read it four times, and still don't understand why you find me threatening. Threatening to what? I never felt that you thought of me that way, but the way you explain it, I can understand why you do. I'm flattered, not put off. And no, it doesn't mean we should no longer correspond.

If I am complicating your life, I am sorry. I never meant to.

I am very confused when you write you're "drawn to a person but repelled by an idea." Yes, I felt the same vibes when we saw each other, but they don't make me nervous. In fact, they make me feel good.

I wish I could make you understand exactly what that means for me.
Even when I was your office assistant, you were always this unap-
proachable teacher-type person, completely controlled, knowing, and
enormously sensitive. For me to have you tell me that you can't think of
me as a kid anymore . . . that's wonderful. I've never thought of you as
"some doddering old busybody," and when I read about your feelings
of being trapped, I cried. You're neither old nor trapped, Tom.

But when you write about me as some tempting symbol of escape, I
could scream. It's fine being a person, rotten being a symbol.

If you come up to see the performance, I don't know what will
happen, either. I don't plan things like that. They either happen or they
don't. But I don't think that if I slept with you the consequences would
be excruciating for me. Where did you get such an idea? It sounds so
horribly conceited that I can't believe that you wrote that. I really
can't. It has to be an excuse. Just what are you afraid of?

I'm not "a plastic mind." God, you can be maddening. Can't you
just come up here and let things flow? You may feel differently; I may
feel differently. I would hate to lose you as a friend. Friends *do* visit.
You're not "compelled to culminate intellectual intimacy with physical
intimacy." Shit. That's just shit.

I think you cover your feelings with a blanket of vocabulary. What
are you afraid of? We aren't that fragile.

I can't take much more of this. Look, if you're coming, it's the last
weekend of the month. Every time I get a letter from you I am no good
to anyone for three days.

                                                        Rita

                                              Apr. 3

Just a note to let you know I am thinking of you.

                                              Always,
                                              R.

                                              Apr. 20

Dear Tom,

I hope you haven't written me a letter the dorm people neglected to forward. A bunch of us have rented a house near campus. It's this really old Victorian mansion with a billion rooms and windows. We've divided housekeeping duties. There are eight of us and I love them all.

The weekend you were here was beautiful. I know you feel the same way. Nicest is that now, a month later, I still feel the same warmth for you—I mean the same warmth I felt for you before the weekend. It was three days I will always remember as special and apart. Nothing has changed for me. You see, I'm not "plastic."

You're still my best friend and I hope you will write me a letter soon. Tell me how things are. What are you doing? School has only six weeks to go. A few of the people I am living with are talking about driving across the country. I'll go, or I might stay here if I can get some work. There's a chance I can assist a Dance Therapist. I won't be in the city at all, so I won't be able to see you, although I'd like to. Just to talk again, as we used to. Nothing has to get complicated.

Write. Please.

Love,
Rita

May 12

Dear Tom,

My mother is sick in PR and they want me to go down there. I can't go until after finals. If I go, I'm scared I'll never get back. I don't know what to do. If momma is in hospital my brothers and sisters need me, and I will go. This year I learned and grew so much, I know there will never be another year like it, but if I go, I will lose it all.

We're being kicked out of the mansion. None of us is old enough to sign a lease, and we've had some terrible fights, petty things that make no sense. Everything is falling apart. I guess I was meant to be alone.

I'm terribly afraid your silence is because you want distance between us. Can't things be as they were? I had you once as a lover. Do I have to lose you as a friend? I swear, Tom, I never planned anything. I swear. What is it? Do you feel guilty? Was I no good? What? Tell me, or don't if you can't, but please write.

I'm frightened. A little letter. I'm suffering and I need a friend. I need you. Please.

Love,

Rita

Nov. 15

Dear Mr. Burnam:

I put no return address on the envelope because I want to be sure you open it. I thought of you this afternoon when I was throwing out some stuff and I came across my high school yearbook. I read what you wrote. Then I threw it out.

Mother passed away last July. I've been taking care of my father and my brothers and my sisters here on the island. I'm seeing a fellow who works in my father's shop. He's considerate and practical, studying to be an electrician. It's pretty much understood we'll marry as soon as the mourning year is finished. I've come to realize that many of the ideas I once had are unrealistic. We do not need courage so much as we need dedication. We need foresight more than we need spontaneity. Last year seems like someone else's dream.

I think I understand why you never wrote to me, and I do not want you to write now. You're free of that obligation. If I caused you any pain, I am sorry, and as for me, none of that matters anymore. You were really never just another one, though.

I'm writing this to be certain you know that. But not from any sense of kindness, Tom.

Do think of me sometimes.

Sincerely yours,

Rita Montanez

The Last Game

"Aces over fives."

"You can't bluff me. Three sixes," she said and her arms curled about the small pile of chips and gathered them across the green felt.

We were sixteen. The final afternoon we played poker together we were once again in the garage behind Bernie's house. Bernie's father had fixed the place up. There was a bathroom with a door, a workbench, tools neatly arrayed on the walls, three bare lights dangling from the ceiling, and a hexagonal poker table. We liked the felt surface—it made us feel "professional"—and Bernie's father had poker chips, which were convenient. We never had to show up with pockets bulging with coins but could simply exchange bills for chips. Bernie kept the bills in a cigar box on the workbench near the bathroom.

Sheila was one of the guys, but not so you'd notice. She was the only girl in the group, and none of us thought that was peculiar. She played a tight game of cards. We'd more or less grown up together in the neighborhood, a nicer part of the city, and in the way kids do we took for granted each other's constant presence, assuming such would last forever. Sheila had always been there, as profane as any of us, and she was an athlete. She swam on the school team, and so she moved with that unthinking confident certainty of the trained athlete I have always envied. She was no tomboy, though. An athletic boy is always aware of his body—it's his calling card—and so he moves with stolid deliberation, and he dresses to advertise himself. You know the type: tight T-shirt, team jacket with a large letter. But Sheila moved lithe as a dancer with none of a dancer's theatricality, and she dressed simply; a slightly too large white shirt, the sleeves rolled over her elbows, and sky-blue jeans. Her straw-yellow hair was cropped short, for the swimming I guess, and she was pretty in a straightforward way. She managed to be feminine without guile. The other girls we knew were always testing themselves, and so putting us to the test, too. The flirting, the giggling, a girl's touch on your hand—all of it filled us with unbearable tension. I don't blame them, the girls, now as I try to recall how it was. I know, of course, that I and the other boys, by an offhand gesture, a careless word or a challenging glance created as much—probably more—anguish for the girls. That's just the way it was; placing blame is stupid.

I knew none of that then, naturally, but I did know—and I believe the other four fellows at the table also knew—that Sheila was special. None of that tension had ever been around her, none of that supercharged atmosphere of possibilities, possibilities wanted and feared. I had my fantasies about her, of course, and I am sure the other fellows did too, but where my fantasies about other girls were swift and anatomical, my dreams of Sheila were soft and scenic. She was fine without being pristine, and it was good for us to believe a woman could be like that. It made us better.

That last May afternoon, we played poker for a few hours. All of us were near even or winning a little, except Bernie who'd lost five dollars, a lot of money for us then. You could see he was disappointed at his luck, but he was a good loser and made no complaint when we agreed it was getting late, near dinner, and time to call the game. While we counted our chips, he retrieved the cigar box from the workbench, placed it on the table's center, and opened it.

The box was empty.

We looked at each other, nervously smiled, then giggled, unwilling to believe that one of us could be a thief. Someone said, "Big joke. We're hysterical. Come on, whoever is the comic, put it back," but no one moved. No one had come in or gone out of the garage while we'd played, but each of us had at one time or another gone to the bathroom, passing the cigar box on the workbench. With the others intent on the game, it would have been a simple matter to pocket the bills unseen.

We sat in awkward silence.

"This is bullshit," Bernie said. "How much was there?"

Each of us had taken two dollars worth of chips, and Bernie had taken three dollars more. Fifteen dollars.

"Man, I don't like this."

"A joke is a joke, but enough is. . . ."

"I don't think it's a joke," I said.

"Why don't we turn out the lights?" Sheila said, then explained she'd seen a movie once where that was what they did to give a thief a chance. It seemed a good idea, so we all stood and Bernie pulled each of the lights' chains. There were no windows in the garage except for the one in the bathroom, and that was covered by a piece of plywood, so the garage was perfectly dark. We could hear each other breathe, each of us absolutely still, listening for the slightest sound of movement. After a few minutes, Bernie pulled the chain of the single bulb directly over the table. The bulb swung, casting a harsh light and garish shadows across our faces. The cigar box was still empty.

"Shit."

Sheila laughed. "That's what happened in the movie. Now we all join the Foreign Legion."

"Oh, shut up," Bernie said, and Sheila shrugged her slim shoulders.

"Why don't we just forget it," I said. "Just go home."

"Not a chance. We're getting to the bottom of this," Bernie said hotly. The guys mumbled agreement.

We were still standing in our places about the table. "Nobody move," a fellow said. "Freeze. Everybody, right now, turn your pockets inside out." We did. Keys, some change, wallets—which we searched—all sorts of junk, fell to the table. No one had more than three dollars. We examined each other's back pockets. Nothing.

I knew it wouldn't work.

"Okay," the same guy said, his voice cracking, "take off your shoes."

We stepped from our shoes, actually sneakers for most of us.

"Socks, too."

We peeled our socks from our feet.

"Phew! Stinks in here," a guy said, but nobody laughed.

"This floor is disgusting," Sheila said, and walked over to the workbench. She easily boosted herself up and sat on it, hugging her knees. Her toes wiggled. The bottoms of her bare feet had been dirtied by the floor. I felt sorry for that.

I suggested that we search the garage, hoping they would find the money and we'd be done with it. I didn't want to be the one to find the bills. That wouldn't look right. We searched in pairs to keep it honest, looked everyplace, but no one looked in the toilet tank. So we stood glaring at each other, knowing some of us would catch hell for getting home so late, but we were snared.

I wish I could say I'd placed a rubber band around the bills and attached them to the toilet float arm because I needed the money, that my father was out of work or something like that, but that would not be true. I just did it. To see. It was easier than I thought. I've never stolen money since then, and the funny thing is I never got to use that fifteen dollars. For all I know, the bills are still there if they haven't rotted.

So we stood there. But it was too late to pass it off as a joke, and I was not about to confess and lose my friends. I'd dealt this hand and now I had to play.

"I guess that's it," a fellow said.

"No, dammit," Bernie said. "There's one more thing. We strip."

And we all turned to Sheila, huddled on the workbench where she seemed tiny. I remember how cool she was, just one eyebrow cocked and her lips thinned, but she didn't say a word. I became ashamed and looked away, and I noticed the other boys did the same. She was our friend, the girl unlike the others, and we did not want to lose that. The stakes had grown high and events had taken their own direction. She *was* different, had to be considered differently, and in that moment we'd turned as one to Sheila, we regretfully knew it.

"Why don't we forget it," I said to Bernie. "Hell, you were the loser. None of the money was yours, anyway."

"That's not the point," he said and pulled his sweatshirt over his head. He held it in his hand, challenging us.

I glanced at Sheila. She had not moved, but her pale eyes were sad. As the other guys and I stripped to our waists, I watched her. Her eyes narrowed, became hard pins of defiance. You could see she'd reached a decision. She would not cry; the best touch football halfback on the block was too tough for that. She jumped easily from the workbench and went to her place at the table where her shoes and socks were.

For a second, I was grateful. I thought she was going to leave, and that would take me off the hook. I am sure that if she made to go, none of us would have tried to stop her. But she did not leave. She sat on the wooden chair where she'd sat most of the afternoon, sat among us, and she folded her hands across her chest.

"Go ahead," she said, looking at each of us in turn, stabbing us with her eyes. "All of you, first. I didn't take any damn money, and I don't care who did. I don't think any of you care, either. But go ahead. See if you have the nerve."

Bernie first, then the rest of us, one at a time, took off our pants. We stood in our shorts, embarrassed and surprised that we could go through with it. "That's enough," Bernie said, and we all turned to Sheila, still seated.

"You're going to make me do this," she said. It was no question, nor was there a note of astonishment or panic. Her voice was dead level. I had no doubt she would, and I realized the stakes were highest for her. She knew our eyes on her, like this, relentless, would defile her, forever deprive her of the easiness she'd had with us, make her like the others.

We watched her stand. She peered at each of us, not looking for a reprieve, but examining, imprinting on her mind exactly what we were. Her examination was unforgiving, but as her hand went to the first button of her shirt I noticed her tremble. She knew one of us had the power to stop this, and she was gambling that he would have as much courage as she.

I started to say the words, but they died in my throat. She unfastened her shirt, enduring our probing eyes. The animal heat in the garage was palpable. As she had been our friend, we had been hers, but that was finished now, lost to her, and I had lost it, too. We watched her hard.

She slipped her arms from the shirt and placed it on the back of the chair, but it fell to the floor. Her skin was very fair, her brassiere very white. She unsnapped the waistband of her jeans and undid the fly, keeping her eyes on us as she pushed her pants below her hips. There was no sound but our breathing. She had to bend to step out of her pants, and I remember how the knuckles of her spine moved beneath her skin. She wore sheer bikini panties, the dark triangle between her thighs plainly visible.

"Okay," Bernie said. "Stop." His voice rasped.

"Screw you. Screw you all," Sheila whispered and reached behind her to the clasp of her bra. It slid down her arms. She gripped it in her fist and shook it. "No money. No goddam money," she said, and with absolute dignity, as though none of us was there, she dressed. A streak of oily grit slanted across the front of her shirt. Without another word or a glance back she went through the door and left us.

"Nice tits," Bernie said. "Nice tits."

They had to tear me off him.

Singing on the *Titanic*

Shortly after my mother's death, my father took me out of school for a week of skiing. We flew into Denver where we were met by a shuttle bus that carried us farther west and higher into the Rockies. It was late March and we had fine weather, sun-dazzling glare off sparkling slopes, the sky at the horizon pale blue deepening overhead to rich purple, a sky I could not know from our home on the flat coast of North Carolina. However, the morning we loaded our luggage aboard the hotel van for the return trip to the airport, the sky boiled with pewter gray clouds, and a penetrating damp wind gusted from the north. Through the van's windshield I watched my father and the hotel driver, their hands deep in the rear pockets of their jeans, sheep-lined fleece collars raised about their necks as they eyed the heavens. I'd fallen in love with the driver when he'd greeted us at the airport—tall and lean, a shock of blonde hair that fell from beneath his Stetson over his eyes—but he was never to know that. Nor would he learn that two days later my affections had flown to the ski instructor in blue stretch pants, a devotion I maintained in exquisite silence for the remainder of our stay. I was fifteen then, and fell in love instantly and completely, an uncomplicated state of affairs I now wish I could recapture, but I have grown cautious.

Halfway to Denver the snow began, at first as soft as a blessing but then with greater vehemence, and gradually the world became diminished by the eerie silence common only to snow. At the airport there was no longer any wind to speak of, but flakes as large as my thumbnail fell in billows heavy with moisture. As the driver placed our luggage on the terminal curbside and the bags were wheeled off by a redcap, the driver reassured my father that these folks in Denver were used to this sort of thing and there was no doubt our plane would get off the ground.

As he slipped the strap of his totebag over his shoulder, my father asked, "You're that certain?"

"You bet," the driver said and flashed that laconic smile that had stolen my heart. He touched the brim of his hat by way of farewell, pulled himself into the van, and vanished forever from my life.

At the gate we learned that the plane's departure was to be delayed by thirty minutes, which meant we had a wait of not quite two hours. Through the thick panes of glass, we watched a fleet of six snowplows head from the terminal to the runways, and then they were folded from sight within the curtains of relentless snow.

My father smoked his pipe and read a Denver newspaper. He cocked his good ear up at each public address announcement, but as none of them concerned our flight, he said little. The announcements came with greater frequency: delays in boardings, delays in departures, delays in arrivals.

"Look at this," he said to me and tapped his paper with the stem of his pipe. I read the weather forecast: clear and mild. My father smiled. I smiled in return.

My father was never prone to displays of affection or any other emotion, which is not to say he was an unfeeling man. He and my mother had had three daughters—I was youngest by six years—and so he had had few opportunities to share with his family his enthusiasms: hunting, fishing, hiking, and so forth. Though I remember when I was very young all of us being packed tightly into our station wagon along with tents, rods and reels, Coleman stoves, and other sports gear, it was clear to me even as young as I was that those family expeditions were undertaken by my mother and sisters more as toleration for my father's eccentricities than out of any true spirit of togetherness. I suppose my father was disappointed in having only daughters. My sisters each went off to high school cheerleading, college, and finally to marriage, in a way permanently pardoning themselves from those pastimes my father loved. He spent an annual solitary week in the Great Smokies, times I chiefly remember for my mother's sipping late-night coffee in our dark kitchen each night until his return. So my father was a very private man, taciturn and controlled, qualities likely assets to him as a probate attorney but which to me made him primarily a figure of some mystery and unfathomable strength. His iron demeanor at my mother's funeral was mistaken by many for shock, but I was certain my father drew upon some inner resource unknowable to the rest of us, a resource I at once envied and thought indecent, as darkly attractive and forbidding as the wilds he so loved.

My father was slapping out the last of his second pipe against his palm when our plane began boarding. We claimed the forward bulk-head seats he'd been careful to reserve for us even before our departure from home. A tall man, he valued legroom. After stowing his totebag in the overhead compartment he checked my seatbelt by tugging at it, and then he helped himself to three magazines. While I studied every move of the stewardess as she went through her choreographed routine to prepare us for disaster, my father studied the copy of *Fortune* he'd placed in his lap. Though we would be flying at thirty thousand feet, I nevertheless felt some reassurance knowing the precise location of each emergency exit, the shape of our oxygen masks, and that my seat cushion would float in the event we plummeted into the Mississippi River or the Potomac, the only two bodies of water I was certain we were to pass over.

Outside, snow steadily fell. With a great rumble the plane began to move. We sat in arctic isolation at the head of a runway for nearly an hour, and then the pilot tersely informed us that our wings had accumulated too much weight. The air aboard the plane had grown fetid; the passengers sat silent except for an infant somewhere in the rear.

As the plane lumbered back to its point of origin, my father touched a passing stewardess's wrist.

"Will we be taking off?"

She said she believed so, though no one could be certain of these things in this kind of weather. Spring storms are the worst because they are unexpected, she said, smiled professionally, and turned from us, and for a moment I wondered if my plans to become a microbiologist might be postponed a few years so I might for a short while roam the skies while wearing a uniform as stylish as hers. But when I glanced at my chest, I decided with some resignation that the lab coat better suited my talents.

Back within the terminal, we watched the storm. My father pointed out to me that no one made any effort to remove snow and ice from the plane's wings. Other craft, arrayed against the terminal like so many suckling pigs against a sow, were dark, emptied of their passengers, cold and lifeless. Stillness gripped the airport. During the next half-hour we heard one plane land—the sound muffled and far off—and we heard none ascend, so we were not surprised to be informed that our official departure had been rescheduled for two hours later yet.

Denver's is a busy airport, and I had been delighted to partake of the sense of purpose and rush of the people within it, but now there was less movement, though there were more people. The air smelled of wet wool and human perspiration, and perhaps we spoke in whispers in unconscious acknowledgment of the snowstorm's quiet power which had leveled us all—business travelers, tourists, students—to the status of those who can only wait. One-time-laughing skiers stood listlessly, leaning against walls. The California beach-bound with their children huddled closer to one another. Fleshy, slack-jawed businessmen, rumpled as their polyester suits, curled into impossible positions on plastic seats and slept. The jeans-and-cowboy-hat crowd had already found a bar and were engaged in an impromptu party. The men's mustaches frosted with the foam of beer, and I envied the young women that so easily tolerated the arms of what I imagined to be strangers going about their waists. And I saw with some despair the long line of women waiting for their chance for the lavatory. My father noticed no one wearing any airline insignia was to be seen.

"They're away," he said. "Hiding in locker rooms or lounges, I imagine." He touched the bulge of his pipe in his pocket, hesitated, and I saw in his eyes the decision made to delay filling it. Then he ran his fingers through his thinning hair. "Come on," he said. "We have work to do."

"What?"

"Get ready. Make plans."

"For what? Can't I go to the bathroom at least?"

He seemed not to hear me, or more likely simply chose not to, a response my sisters and I were long familiar with. Later, when I thought about it, I could not recall any time he'd treated my mother in that fashion, a fact that pleased me.

He withdrew a ten-dollar bill from his pocket and instructed me to get coins, then wander in search of vending machines. He told me to get what I could, that plastic-wrapped sandwiches were best, turkey especially, but to avoid anything spread with mayonnaise. "And don't buy milk, unless you want to drink it right away. Soda pop is fine. And juice. Lots of canned juice."

"We'll be leaving in two hours. They said two hours."

"I doubt it."

"But they *said*."

"They say a lot of things."

"Why don't we just wait and see what. . . ."

"Listen, love. In two hours this place will be picked clean. Buy candy bars. Lots of candy bars." He touched his chin. "And if you see a disposable razor, get that too. Come to think of it, take this." He handed me a second ten.

"Daddy, I can't carry. . . ."

"Your pockets. In your coat. Anyplace you can. That ski jacket is bulky, just draw the waist-string tight."

He laughed. I had not seen him laugh at all recently, not once on the slopes when we'd skied. The sternness around his eyes for a very short moment dispersed like fog in the sun. When I went to hug him he stepped backward.

"Come on, now. We've got important things to do."

"You make it sound like we'll be here for days."

He looked out the window to where the snow fell.

"Could be," he said softly and touched my forehead. His unaccustomed touch, a kind of apology, felt good, but I could see how the effort had cost him. "And I'll be . . . ," he glanced around, ". . . over there." He pointed at a bank of telephones. "Try for a motel room. What do you think? About eight inches so far?"

The wind outside was rising. Drifts made it hard to guess. Nothing moved.

"That yo-yo sure didn't know what he was talking about. What's his name? The driver."

"Murphy," I said. "Everybody calls him Murph."

"How do you know that?" I heard my father ask, genuinely surprised, as I went without answering him in search of coins and vending machines.

It took some time. The food and notions stands had long lines and the counter workers were reluctant to give change, but eventually I had ten chocolate bars of varying degrees of nuttiness, six sandwiches of which only one had to be liverwurst, three small containers of orange juice, and my chief prizes, a half-dozen containers of yogurt, three of which were actually blueberry. I'd even managed to find a shaving razor. Carrying all of it in my jacket, I felt like a shoplifting kangaroo.

My father was at a phone, his credit card in hand. He nodded approval at the load I carried, and he replaced the telephone receiver into its claw as I approached.

"That's enough for me," he said. "Seven strikes and you're out. One fellow told me they promised their last room at eleven this morning. Besides, he said the airport has been officially closed to traffic, air or ground. They won't even allow a taxi in to get us." He took a yogurt and plastic spoon from me. "Any milk?"

"Just juice. You said milk would spoil. Maybe we'll take off when they said."

"Maybe, but I wouldn't count on it. That's a first-class blizzard out there. First-class. Nobody expects it, and it sweeps down out of the mountains." He stared out the window. "Just like that. To remind us." He slowly turned to me and waved his arm in a circle. "We'll stake out some floor as soon as I get my totebag."

"Can't you get a room? Doesn't the airline have a responsibility to us?" I was near tears, less because of the prospect of sleeping on a floor than at the amusement my distress was creating for my father.

"The only person who will take care of you is you. Or me, maybe. So if you haven't slept on a floor, it's time you did. Heck, it's just camping indoors." He began walking away.

I hurried to follow him through the boarding tunnel. He was whistling happily, his unbuttoned jacket flapping about his hips, his step jaunty. A lone stewardess greeted us at the plane, my father showed her our tickets, explained why we were there, and she allowed us aboard.

In the overhead compartment where my father had stowed his bag were two pillows and blankets. He rolled them carefully under his arm after taking the sandwiches and other food from me and cramming them into the bag. As we went to leave the plane the stewardess stopped him and sweetly explained that passengers might not deboard with blankets or pillows.

"You know we'll be in the terminal all night?"

"We *are* scheduled to depart in about an hour, sir."

When my father looked out the port to the graying world, the stewardess's eyes followed his. "Now, you don't believe that, do you?"

She chewed her lip and I saw the professional glaze leave her eyes. My father, I realized from the lilt in his eyes and carriage, was enjoying himself.

"Company policy. . . ."

"Bull." I'd never before heard my father interrupt anyone but his children, so when he snapped at her I was as shocked as she. "I don't give a rat's ass for company policy. I am getting off this plane with these things and the only question is just what you can do about it. I promise you that we will return them when we finally do get aboard this plane. You have my word. They do no one any good locked up in that compartment, and they will do me enormous good in the terminal, so I mean to take them with me. If you think you must do something to stop me, you are invited to try."

He spoke very calmly. My heart was hammering. I had never seen him like this, and it was a revelation to me of just what he was capable, a different man than any I had supposed, direct, determined, and uncaring who knew it.

The professional glaze returned to her eyes as she played her trump, what I could tell from her voice she believed to be an unassailable argument, one that forever would put my father in his proper place.

"And what if all our passengers want blankets? We don't have enough."

"Then it's too damned bad for them, isn't it?"

He walked by her.

I paused a moment, caught by the impulse to apologize to her, but I saw she was not all that upset. Her hair was bedraggled and coming loose from the bun into which it had been pinned, and there were great semicircular stains ringing the sleeves of her blouse. Somewhere, I imagined, someone she could not join waited for her. The storm had trapped her, too. Then I realized my father was already passing through the tunnel and was about to return to the terminal. I ran to catch him.

He must have heard my steps, for he said without turning to look at me, "Don't misunderstand what you just saw. I'd have said the same thing to a man. Or a group of men, for that matter."

I wondered that he felt he had to say that to me. When he turned to look at me, I lowered my eyes.

"You think I was cruel?"

"No."

"Crude, then? Overbearing?"

"Maybe. What if everybody *did* want one?"

"Then we'd be damned fools not to get them first. This isn't some schoolyard where you can't have bubble gum unless you brought enough for everybody."

We looked about the terminal. A fellow sat cross-legged on the floor, a guitar in his lap, surrounded by several people who clapped and sang. A bridge game was in progress, and near the foursome a small boy played chess with a man that might have been his grandfather.

"You have to be ready for anything," he said. "Don't let appearances fool you. They sang on the *Titanic*."

He led me to a few vacant square feet of floor over which he spread the small blankets. Though I still needed the lavatory, it was clear that this was not a moment I could leave him. There was more to be said. I'd have asked him if he thought we were on the *Titanic*, but I suddenly knew him, and knew that, yes, he believed we were. Always.

I sat on the blanket beside him when he tugged at my hand. Slowly, precisely, he peeled the cellophane from a sandwich and gave me half.

"In '51 I was in Korea," he said, though he seemed to be talking more to himself than to me. "I was on leave in Okinawa once, and on my way back to country couldn't get off the ground because of rain. You've never seen rain like that. As though a faucet had been left on.

Astonishing. Three days." He took a small sip of orange juice. "We waited in this airplane hangar, just a huge metal shed with a concrete floor, and it was as hot and humid as any place you can imagine. Well, the place filled with G.I.'s. Air Force, Navy—the lot. So it just got hotter and hotter in that place. There was just one toilet, and I guess there were two hundred men in there. No one could leave. We were afraid the rain would let up while we were gone and we'd miss a cargo plane headed for Seoul, and so catch all kinds of hell for being AWOL. No place to lie down but a concrete floor. Nothing to eat except for whatever you happened to be carrying. To amuse ourselves we'd strip and dance naked in the rain, except that got to be dangerous because there was an excellent chance that when you got back inside your shoes would be missing."

"Why wasn't there any food?"

"You don't understand the Army. Heck, the Army doesn't understand the Army. You see, we were all from different outfits, which in the Army means we were no one's responsibility. Just so many bodies in transit. Half the men in the place had no papers, just thumbed a ride, and now they were stuck where they were. Since no one *had* to feed us, no one did. I suppose after a while they'd have worked something out, but it was easier to hope that at any moment the rain would stop and the problem would disappear."

"Sounds awful."

"Well, if you like poker it wasn't so bad. You want another sandwich?"

I shook my head.

"I did all right," he said and zipped the bag shut. "I had three cases of beer I was bringing back to the men in my outfit. Budweiser. So I held onto the stuff—sat on it, actually—while I played cards the whole first day. By the second day those beers were worth quite a lot. Warm and all, at least they were wet."

"You sold them?"

"No. Why should I do a thing like that? I traded. You want a beer? What have you got to eat? Two beers for a clean shirt. I got half a bar of soap for one beer, and that was the best deal I made because after that I could rent the soap." He laughed, and his eyes were truly merry.

I had to smile. "There was a marine from Oklahoma who was getting on the nerves of a navy man from Texas . . . , well, never mind. You can imagine." He finished his orange drink.

I was fascinated by the story, as far as I knew the first anyone had ever heard such a thing from him, and I was also somewhat unsettled by it. All I'd ever known of his time in the service was a tattered black-and-white photograph of him in an Eisenhower jacket, lean and young and I think handsome, his peaked hat pulled a trifle too far forward over his forehead. The photo stood in a gilt frame on the bureau in his bedroom beside the formal portrait of my mother and him on their wedding day. None of it fit with the man I knew, a man impossible to envision playing marathon poker, drinking beer, and dancing naked in the rain.

"So you made a lot of money?"

"No. I told you. No money. I wouldn't get rich at it. That would have been indecent, I think. I only traded for what I needed. It was just one of those situations that reminds you of what you really need—food, shelter, clothing. Basics. That's what you have to be ready for. Why you go up into the hills. You just never know what will happen next. You just have to be ready." I wondered if my mother had ever understood exactly why he'd gone into the mountains. "You sure you don't want another sandwich?" he asked.

I said I would save it for later, and he nodded, lapsed into silence, and withdrew his pipe from his pocket, a familiar enough sign to me that he wished to be left alone.

As I stood finally to go to the lavatory, he gestured that I should bend close enough to him that he could whisper. "Take some extra toilet tissue. And if there are paper towels, get as many as you can."

That night I smoked my first cigarette, given to me by a young woman—perhaps she was twenty-eight—named Altina. She had silken long dark hair that cascaded over her face and shoulders when she threw back her head to laugh, which was frequently. I'd given her the liverwurst sandwich, and by way of exchange she told me thrilling tales about the men in her life, their inconstancies and her own betrayals. I thought her wonderful. She'd never had to work, yet led a life of opulent movement. I spent much of the night with a pack of people my own age wandering through the terminal in search of shadow places.

We giggled a great deal, and I was mad for a blue-eyed boy named Roger. I allowed Roger to kiss me, but his life was to be in Chicago and mine was to be elsewhere.

And so that long night in the terminal, I did not sleep at all, but that was my choice.

My father spent the night in relative comfort, beneath a blanket, his head resting on a pillow. In the morning the sun rose bright, and we saw the mountains to the west gradually illuminated and shining with new snow. My father shaved, and we were able to wash with the last of the purloined paper towels. Refreshed, clean, we breakfasted on the last two yogurts, and by lunch we were aloft into the cloudless sky. Our fellow passengers were bag-eyed and weary, spiritually as wrinkled as their clothes. My father, however, was buoyant, and I loved him for that, but nevertheless, when I felt the eyes of the other passengers on us, I suffered embarrassment and guilt.

Some weeks later, my father began to date. My delighted sisters spent a small fortune on long-distance calls to me. Our phone hung on a kitchen wall.

"What is this one like?"

"I don't know. I didn't see her."

"Well, what time did they get back?"

"Dad came home by himself. Don't be gross."

"When?"

"When what?"

"When did he get back?"

"Two. About two." I took a winesap apple and saw that I would soon need to scrub the refrigerator's interior.

"Two! That's wonderful. You stayed up?"

"Did not." I bit the apple. "Was watching a movie. Monster ate Japan."

"You've got to get a look at her. Work on it. How many times has he gone out with this one?"

"That's spying. Why don't you ask Dad yourself?"

"Now how could I do that? You do wait up for him, though."

"Don't."

"Do."

"Don't."

My sisters and I had over the years developed conversational patterns that reduced otherwise intelligent women to the verbal abilities of the inhabitants of a sandbox.

"You've got to try this time. Did he tell you where he met her?"

"No."

"Ask!"

They were those kinds of conversations. I ate a good many apples, but I told my sisters very little because by that time I had completely become my father's ally.

Actually, as I recall, the first time my father dated a woman, he'd been maneuvered by his law partner into escorting a lady to a dinner party. Keeping me company at our kitchen table, he smoked two pipes while I picked at something breaded I'd defrosted. He was overeager to serve me. A second glass of milk? Fruit? All this was extraordinary.

After I'd eaten and the dishes were done, he asked that I check his shirt collar properly covered his tie. I remember the rigid stiffness of the starched material beneath my fingers, and that I patted his shoulder.

We were in his bedroom, and we peered into the mirror above the bureau. "You look fine," I said. "Can I go now?"

"Wait a bit."

I stood beside the bureau and my hand touched its glossy surface. Nothing was on it but the photo of my father in his army uniform and a new bottle of cologne, I suppose the only bottle of cologne he'd ever obtained that was not a gift. I watched him change from a white shirt to a blue one, reject that and disappear into his walk-in closet to return with a yellow shirt, and finally settle on the white shirt with which he'd begun. The tie was always a solid navy blue.

"What are you nervous about?"

"I'm not nervous. Do I look nervous?"

"It's just a dinner."

He moved further from me and straightened his tie. "Do you think I'm doing the right thing?" There was a long moment while we looked at each other's reflections. "I mean, wearing a suit. Is it the right thing?"

So I left his room and found some homework I could do, but I could not get myself to concentrate on the text, something about the organization of the Anglican Church and the policies of Henry VIII.

My father found me curled into the corner of our living room sofa. He leaned a shoulder against the door frame, looking as near perfect as ever in his three-piece pinstripe suit. I could smell sweet cologne fresh on his raw-shaved cheek.

"Why don't you have a girlfriend come over and keep you company?" he asked.

"I'll be fine."

"You could go to a movie. Call someone. I'll drop both of you at the mall."

He shifted his weight and leaned his shoulder against the wall. I saw his shoes were not polished, and for a moment I thought I would tell him that, but it seemed too cruel.

"I'll be fine right here."

"Well, I'm off."

I nodded.

He waited a heartbeat, but since I had returned my attention to the book in my lap there was nothing more that could be said. I heard him go to the garage and I heard him start the engine of his new car, a low growl, nothing at all like the cranky whining ignition of the station wagon that for years my mother had driven until that clear evening a pick-up had sailed over the divider and snuffed out her life.

The hush of the empty house enfolded me. When King Henry appropriated church lands, I closed the book and turned on the television. I thought how if my father were to go out again I would want to say something to him about his cologne, and I thought how I should have this evening said something about his shoes.

Eventually I went up to my room and lay on my soft bed. In the dark stillness I listened to the sounds of an empty house, those mysterious creaks and bumps we tell ourselves are the products of thermal expansion and contraction but in the night make of a house a live thing in which we are permitted only temporarily to reside. Then, sometime later, just after midnight, earlier than I'd expected, I heard the rattle of our garage door, the growl of my father's car, the clink of keys as he worked the burglar alarm, his muffled footsteps on the carpeted stair, and I saw his shadow shape pass by my half-open door.

I do not know why I expected him to stop at my room—that was certainly never his habit—but after a few minutes when it became clear he would not, I felt compelled to slip into my robe, and barefoot I walked softly down the hall. The golden light of his nightstand lamp fell through his bedroom doorway, and I stood beyond the edge of that oblong of cast light.

My father sat at the corner of his huge bed, his profile toward me. He seemed weary, heavy as a statue cast in bronze. His jacket was rumpled carelessly where it had been flung across an armchair, and his unbuttoned vest hung limply from his rounded shoulders. His tie was pulled from his throat and dangled into the space above his lap. I saw where he had opened a bureau drawer and taken out the wedding portrait of him and my mother, and he held it in his two hands, his elbows braced on his knees, and he wept. His body shook with it.

"Helpless," he whispered. "Helpless."

I wanted to go to him, but I knew I should not. If my arm were to supportively encircle his slack shoulders, they would stiffen and he would take refuge within the fortress of his presumed self-sufficiency. So as I silently passed again through the dark hushed house to my tiny room, I saw that even for a man like my father, in the face of it, at the end, there was no preparation possible, no amount of strength that was sufficient, and I saw that I could love him the more for that, knowing that within his solitude he trembled.

ILLINOIS SHORT FICTION